This one is for
Ray Bradbury
and
Rod Serling . . .
for opening the door
when I was very young.

The pilgrimage is one that each of us must make alone, into the realm of the stars and galaxies, to the limits of the universe, to that boundary of space and time where the heart and mind encounter the ultimate mystery, the known unknowable. It is a pilgrimage in quest of the soul of the night.

—Chet Raymo

PROLOGUE

Mister Magister was not his real name.

But that was not important. Nor were his origins as special as his purpose—to search for certain qualities in living things. Sentient things. His quest, his mission, was eternal.

As if gathered up from the shadows of darkness, taking form and substance under the cold, white heat of a midwestern night sky, he appeared. His body was long and thin, emaciated further by the dark clothing he wore: black pants and jacket, black string tie upon a wrinkled white shirt. About his shoulders hung a flowing black cape with a high-cowled collar. It was held by a clasp made of silver, in the shape of a claw wrapped about a globe. His face was gaunt, sunken, and very pale; his lips thin and without color, little more than a slash below his hawkish nose. So sunken in his skull were his eyes that they resembled wells driven into shadow, portals into utter darkness. His hair was also black, and plastered thinly to his head, almost invisible beneath his drooping, broad-brimmed hat.

As if a relic of an earlier time, Magister rode atop a long black carnival wagon, pulled by a horse of immense proportions. Jet-black, broad-shouldered, and thickly muscled, the stallion pulled its load with a diffident air. Its gait was a gliding, effortless passage through the night.

He traveled a rural, two-lane road, in a land of waving wheat and ripened corn. The fields, which gauntleted the road, shimmered and moved like a ghostly sea under moonlight. Magister looked up, into the crisp, clean sky, and sensed the coming of the season called autumn.

The time and the town were close at hand.

CHAPTER 1

September in Brampton, Iowa: second crops of corn bleaching and husking in a brassy sun; boys at Nelson's Field dusting through at least one more game of hardball; the Brampton Kiwanis Band struggling through a final Saturday concert at the town square gazebo; the men at Alice Kirstin's boardinghouse savoring one of summer's final pitchers of tinkling lemonade; volunteers at the firehouse sitting out front in straight-back chairs, arguing about George Brett and Eddie Murray.

The baking oven-heat of summer still lingered over the small town during the shortening days. Evenings brought the first hints of the new season —cool breezes and the brittle smells of drying leaves.

It was a time of changes, thought Stella Chambers as she walked down Center Street toward the County Library. Baseball season was drawing to a close, harvest was almost over, school would be starting in another week, and she would be in the tenth grade. Greens would surrender to yellow, orange, and brown, and the blue skies would slide into gray. It was a time when life would begin to change subtly and slowly, and you would be doing new and different things. She wondered, as she walked along, if anybody else sensed the coming changes as pointedly as she.

As she passed Myers' Luncheonette, she forced herself to look inside, past the yellowed-plastic sunshades, where the kids from school were always lounging over ice-cream sodas. Tom Whittington was there. And so were Joel Walker and Mary Atkins. Stella looked away without recognizing any of the other faces. She did not belong in there with that crowd; she knew it, but had always had trouble accepting the fact. For some reason, known only to the young, certain adolescents were accepted while others were not. Stella did not fit in, and sometimes the pain of that knowledge became too much, and she found herself disliking the others. She didn't understand them, and couldn't respect them, but there was a secret part of her that wished to be with them, to be like them. Sometimes it did not matter that they got poor grades in school, or that they were loud and childish, because they seemed to be enjoying life. They were like what Mrs. Tennyson called "comic relief" in those plays by Shakespeare, thought Stella, and sometimes she wished that she could be a part of it. But no one had ever taken the time to teach her any of the dances they were doing at the Rec Center, and she had been afraid to ask. She didn't really like the music they listened to on that loud radio station from Davenport, and her Aunt Leah had expressly forbidden her to wear makeup to school.

Sometimes Stella felt that those things were not important anyway, but there were other times when she thought that maybe they were. She simply was not sure of lots of things these days.

It was a time of changes; it certainly was.

She entered the town square where the Kiwanis Band members were packing up their instruments and tugging uncomfortably at the tight collars of their braided uniforms. No more John Philip Sousa till next year. The spiked shadow of the First Lutheran Church's steeple lay halfway across the square, and the benches were sparsely occupied by people reading newspapers, talking idly, playing checkers. It was a slow, warm, insect-buzzing day, and everyone seemed content to let it slide away.

Crossing the square, Stella entered the library to be engulfed by its cool shadows. She hoped that Jamie might be there. Ever since July, when she had unexpectedly met him in the reading room, the two had been spending afternoons quietly reading and talking. Sometimes they would go down to the luncheonette for cherry Cokes.

His full name was Jamie Rodin, pronounced like the French sculptor's, but many of his classmates bowdlerized it to "rodent." He, like Stella, was not a member of the elite, but it did not seem to bother him as it sometimes did Stella. Jamie seemed too wrapped up in the pursuit of knowledge and discovery to be concerned with belonging. For the past two years he had reached the state finals of the High School Science Fair competition, and he was already researching his next project. He was just about the most interesting person Stella had ever met, including Mr. Weston, who ran the weekly newspaper; Doc Finlay; and even Mr. Strong, who ran the grocery. All of those men were bright and well educated, but they lacked the enthusiasm, the sense of wonder, which radiated from Jamie like sunshine.

Stella had a bagful of memories of all the summer days she had spent with Jamie. After he finished his sweeping and stockwork at Brampton Feed and Hardware, he would join her for trips to the library, walks out past Brampton Depot, or afternoons in the square, where they would sit and trade information from the books they had been reading. Jamie had a photographic memory. He could recite facts about things he'd read as though he still had the pages in front of him; sometimes he could even tell you the number of the page he was talking about. Astronomy, paleontology, biology, physics, and chemistry were his primary interests, but he could still sit and tell you stories about history and geography and anthropology for hours. It seemed to Stella that he knew a little bit about everything.

Jamie was what Aunt Leah called "a nice boy." All you had to do was look at Jamie and you got a good feeling about him. He was tall for his age, very thin and angular. His hair was so brown it looked black, unless he was out in the sun when Stella could see the auburn highlights, and he wore it on the long side because he didn't seem to think much about haircuts. She was glad about that anyway: The new hairstyles looked much too severe to her. She was pleased that Jamie was different in so many ways from the others.

He was on her mind as she entered the general reference room. It was cool and dimly lit, and as her eyes adjusted, she looked to see if Jamie was waiting for her. Old man Waters was sitting in the corner looking at a Rand McNally atlas, and Mrs. Overlea was behind her desk, but otherwise the room was empty. Either she was early or Jamie had extra work at the hardware store and might not be coming by at all. She was disappointed and paused for a moment to think about what that really meant.

It could be, Stella Chambers, that Jamie Rodin is becoming more than just a casual friend, she thought to herself. And she decided that this was acceptable because, after all, it was a time of changes.

As she lay her books on a mahogany table, she wished that she had brought her journal along. It was a thick notebook with the word "Diary" stamped into its imitation-leather cover, but to Stella it was more than a diary. It was a *journal*, a place where she practiced her dreaming and her art, where she worked upon becoming a writer.

Youth, she knew, was *not* wasted on the young, contrary to what some bitter old man had once written. It was the time when the world was still new, and everything in it possessed the seeds of magic—if you only took the time to look for them. It was the time of dreams, the time when dreams could still come true, the time when the fire in your soul was fresh and well banked. Stella's dreams were wrapped up in the lives of women like Emily Dickinson and Sara Teasdale, Isadora Duncan and Eleonora Duse. She was fascinated by these artists of tragic integrity, and wanted to share in their passionate need to write, to dance, to act.

She wanted so much to be like them, freely admitting to herself that she might be an incurable romantic. Like the lives of those she had read, Stella spent hours alone in her gabled bedroom, hunched over her journal, writing within a small island of desk-lamp light. She was a good student, though not as good as Jamie, but she truly excelled in Mrs. Tennyson's English classes, for which she credited the long hours alone with her journal.

Within its pages lay character sketches of Brampton folk, detailing their lives, examining their triumphs and failures. Stella listened to the town gossips with a practiced ear, and wove the fragments she heard into fanciful vignettes. She tried everything from tragedy to poetry to the classic essay. She tried to capture her moods, her opinions, her feelings, and her fears. Within her journal's pages, Stella truly lived. It was the only place where she achieved the freedom of what she believed was the true artist.

Despite the soaring heights she reached while writing, Stella knew how totally subjective this feeling was. She knew how impossible it was to evaluate what she had created, and wished for objective criticism. This desperate need sometimes led her to the brink of temptation—to show her writings to someone else. Although Aunt Leah was the kindest woman Stella had ever known, she knew the old woman would not understand her writing. Worse, Aunt Leah might not even take her writing seriously, deeming it "a phase" that Stella was going through, after which she would "come to her senses." Stella often wondered how many artists had been destroyed by that kind of thinking; or was it perhaps part of the ordeal which must be experienced by *all* creative people?

But how she needed to share her thoughts, her words, with *someone*. She knew that was one of the reasons she was attracted to Jamie Rodin, in whom she sensed a kindred spirit, a person whose view of the world extended beyond the city limits of Brampton, Iowa. She considered this as she sat in the musty coolness of the reference room, remembering how many times she had almost told Jamie about her journal, how many times she had almost asked him to read it. But something had always held her back. Fear? Distrust? Shyness? She did not know.

How silly she was. She imagined herself getting so close to Jamie, and he didn't even know about her special dream! How odd we sometimes are . . .

Time passed and Stella realized that Jamie would not be coming to the library that day. Gathering up her books, she returned them to Mrs. Overlea, then entered the reading room, where all nonreference material was arranged in neat sections and shelves. Lately she had been reading the American Romantics—Emerson and Hawthorne, and, most recently, Poe. It seemed to her that there was special joy in discovering a writer independently, without anyone recommending him to you, and it had been that way with Edgar Allan Poe. She had never heard his name in English class, and then one day, while looking through the adult fiction section, she saw a book of his collected stories. The first tale was "The Tell-Tale Heart," the second, "The Black Cat." Even the titles intrigued her. Stella had been entranced to find such a moody, evocative writer, and had been amazed that no one had ever told her about the dark magic of his prose. She learned that he had written a novel, but she had never been able to find it.

Now she studied the adult fiction section and noticed an intriguing title in boldface: *The Facts of Life and Love,* by Laura Gleesinger. Now, what was *that* doing here? she thought. Probably misshelved.

Stella tilted her head and read the words again, feeling a rush of . . . of excitement? Perhaps. She repeated the words in her mind: *the facts of life . . . and love.*

It *was* a time of changes, she thought as a smile came to her lips. The facts of life. She'd heard the phrase. Even Aunt Leah had said it once, when Stella was preparing for her bath and her godmother brought in fresh towels. "My laws, Stella," she had said, "pretty soon you're going to be a woman. Time soon I sat you down and told you about The Facts of Life."

But that time had never come. Each time Stella asked, Aunt Leah would smile knowingly, make a little clucking sound, and change the subject. It was as though her aunt were teasing her with the forbidden knowledge. Poor Aunt Leah, thought Stella. Her aunt didn't realize that even the junior high school kids were talking about those "facts," that they giggled over them on the playgrounds, in the lavatories, at the luncheonette after school.

The Facts were still a bit of a mystery to Stella, even though she had eavesdropped on conversations, tried to extrapolate meanings from the books she had read. Maybe it was time to clear up the doubts.

Checking to see if anyone was looking, Stella pulled the book from the shelf. It had a coral and tan cover, with a picture of an adolescent boy and girl seated before a genial-looking woman who was presumably in the act of explaining The Facts to the two teenagers. It was odd that she had never noticed the book before, even in the nonfiction sections. It was also strange that she had never sought out such a book, as though she had never thought of such things, and that was untrue. When she checked the due card in the back pocket, she saw that the book had been almost constantly in circulation, and she felt fortunate to have found it. It was like discovering an underground classic. It was a book that seemingly everyone was secretly consulting in a desperate, adolescent need to know the truth.

Stella tucked the book under her arm, pausing to select some other titles: an anthology of American poetry, some stories by Melville, and a book about astronomy. Jamie was always talking about the stars and the planets, and she wanted to read something about them so that they could have more meaningful conversations.

Mrs. Overlea did not attempt to disguise her disapproval of Stella's choice of The Book, but thankfully the woman did not make any comment as she stamped the due date on the much-used card. Stella felt embarrassed enough, and feared that any conversation on the subject would be catastrophic. She left the library hurriedly and walked straight back through town to Madison Street and her aunt's house. The shadows had crept over everything as the afternoon faded into evening, just as summer was giving way to autumn. Soon it would be the time of bloodred harvest moons, hayrides, and Halloween. The streets were emptying of traffic and pedestrians as the shops closed.

Aunt Leah was working in the kitchen when Stella came into the foyer with her books under arm. It was a perfect chance to carry them upstairs to her bedroom and hide The Book in her dresser under her sweaters.

During dinner, Stella found it difficult to maintain an interest in her aunt's conversation. She was anxious to steal away to the privacy of her room and read about Life and Love. So the talk was mostly one-sided as Aunt Leah went on about how school would be starting next week, and how she had so much work ahead of her what with *two* classes of third graders this year. Aunt Leah liked to complain about how those children were going to be her death, but she and Stella both knew that it was a kind of ritual they both went through each autumn. The fact was that Aunt Leah loved those children, and would be lost without her teaching.

She helped her aunt clean the kitchen after dinner, then retired upstairs to read. Aunt Leah remained in the parlor, listening to the radio and working on her quilt, which she claimed would be very much appreciated when "old Jack Frost" came to town. The work would occupy her for several hours, and Stella would be free to read her new book. Since she had discovered it, it had been the only thing on her mind. She was surprised by the urgency building within her. She thought about that and made a note to herself that she would have to comment on her feelings in her journal.

Taking the book from her dresser drawer, she began to read.

Laura Gleesinger had written in a very straightforward style, and there was no condescension in her language or tone. The book was extremely readable and seemed to home in on the feelings and experiences of adolescents. The author stressed the fact that sex was not dirty and that the social taboos associated with it were damaging to the curious young adult. Puberty, read Stella, was an alarming time.

A time of changes, she thought.

In addition to confusing physical changes, there were the added social pressures of peer groups. Fear of rejection, nonacceptance, failure, inadequacy: All were covered in lucid, honest language, and Stella was consumed by the book. She became quickly convinced that her growing sexuality was not something to be feared, that there was nothing dark and brooding or magical about it. She equated it with what the poets often called the "coming of age" or the "loss of innocence." For the first time in her life, she was beginning to understand what those words really meant, and she felt a warmth, a glowing sensation which had never been there before. She didn't want her adolescence to be a painful, bitter experience, and she believed that one way of preventing that would be to understand her sexuality instead of fearing or avoiding it.

The hours passed quickly as she read, pausing only to make notes in her journal or to transcribe a particularly incisive thought, and she did not notice that darkness had settled over the town. Presently, she heard Aunt Leah moving about in her room, preparing for bed. Stella checked her alarm clock and saw that it was very late indeed: so captivating had the book been that she had not taken notice of the hour.

As she undressed, Stella remembered what Laura Gleesinger had said about being aware of your feelings and your body, and how it was a good thing to feel comfortable with both. She stood before the mirror in the warm splash of light from her desk lamp and looked at herself as though she had never actually taken account of her appearance. She saw that her face was getting longer, losing the baby fat, accenting her high, wide cheekbones. Her strawberry-blond hair fell gracefully to her shoulders, unfettered by bows or berets, making a bright, natural frame for her features. Her eyes were a deep sea-green, and looked very large under long lashes. Her nose was small and peppered with freckles, which were beginning to fade like Indian summer. How rosy-colored her lips seemed, not needing lipstick, she thought. When she smiled, it looked natural and sincere. Her neck seemed suddenly more slender, more graceful.

Stepping back from the mirror, she pulled her sweater off, intensely aware of the sensation of the wool gliding over her skin. Taking off her bra, Stella brushed her nipples lightly with her fingertips and they became hard, causing a tingling to rush through her body. She drew off her panties and looked at her nude body in the warm light of her desk lamp. Her whole body was lengthening, becoming slender like a ballerina's. Her small breasts were firm and conical, complementing her new awareness of herself as being on the brink of womanhood. She was pleased to see that her waist was narrowing, stressing the gentle swell of her hips and stomach. Her flesh seemed to almost shimmer with an inner vitality and . . . yes, beauty. She had never really noticed the changes which had been taking place, until now.

Reluctantly, she slipped into a nightgown, before returning to her journal to record her new feelings, her new discoveries about herself.

It was a time of changes, she thought once again.

CHAPTER 2

The sky was touched by evening as the horse-drawn wagon rolled to a silent stop. Mister Magister dropped down from the driver's bench and surveyed the landscape. Yes, he thought calmly, this is where I must be.

His carnival wagon rested in a meadow, just off the shoulder of a road called Route 217, within walking distance of a town called Brampton. Beyond the wagon stood a copse of trees, their leaves drying into autumn colors and rustling in a cool breeze.

Unhitching the black stallion, Magister led it to the copse and tied it to a small elm. It was late afternoon. Time to prepare his Magnificent Gallery.

Very soon now, thought the man in black. Very soon, they would be coming to him.

CHAPTER 3

Billy Parkins, a tow-headed nine-year-old, biked lazily along Route 217. Having just finished his rural deliveries of the *Brampton Bugle,* he was anxious to get home for supper. Billy didn't like doing the paper route, but he did like the money. If he had not accepted the part-time job, he would never have been able to buy the Spaulding infielder's glove—the one with Ozzie Smith's autograph right in the pocket —which now dangled from his right handlebar. Everything had a price, his father always said, and Billy was beginning to understand what that meant.

The two-lane blacktop stretched ahead of him as he pedaled past endless fields of corn and wheat. Ahead, rising above the haze, he could see the rooftops and spires of Brampton. Almost home, he thought, then noticed something unfamiliar on the right side of the road. Some kind of four-wheeled wagon sat there; a man in a cape was working at a panel on the rear. Tied to a tree, a huge black stallion grazed nearby.

Billy pumped his legs, gathering speed, then coasted off the road into the meadow. A carnival wagon, and it was a beauty. About fifteen feet long, maybe six feet wide, it was black as pitch and decked out in fancy white pinstripes, curlicues, and gingerbread. It had brass fittings and filigreed metalwork, and it seemed to Billy to be the most beautiful carnival rig he'd ever seen. In big, majestic gold and white letters across the side panel were the words:

THE MAGNIFICENT GALLERY OF MISTER MAGISTER

Billy read it slowly as the man in black stepped out from behind the wagon to regard him silently.

"Hiya, mister," said Billy, immediately impressed with the man's height, his bearing, and his fancy clothes.

"Good afternoon," said the man, and his voice seemed to linger in the air, like an echo in a big, empty church.

"That's a real fine-lookin' wagon you got there . . ."

"Thank you," said the man, who then continued unlatching the back panel of the wagon. He pulled out the final pin, and the back hinged down to form a countertop suspended by chains on each side.

Billy did not mind the man's quiet manner. He was too intrigued by his strange costume and the elegant wagon. Billy cleared his throat, spoke again.

"You know, we had a carnival through here, 'bout a month ago. Ain't you kinda late, mister? An' where's the rest of the wagons?"

Magister looked up from his work, his eyes burning through the shadow of the hat's brim like glowing coals. "There are no others. I . . . travel alone."

"Alone, huh? Never heard of that before." Billy

paused, his mind racing with excited questions as he tried to order them. "Well, how come you're settin' up outside of town? There's a vacant lot down near the high school . . . you think folks'll come out this far?"

Magister continued to set up the gallery, checking the strength of the chains with a firm tug of his hand. He did not look at Billy as he spoke. "Oh, they will come . . . they will come as far as need be."

Billy climbed off his bike and set the kickstand, taking several cautious steps closer. There was something about the way the man moved, the way he acted, that didn't seem right. His voice was strange; creepy almost. And his clothes—they were *really* something. Billy hadn't seen anybody dressed like that since Logan and Hammerbacker's Circus had set up in nearby Simpsonville, and they had that magician named Spectro in one of the sideshows. But Magister also reminded him of the bad guys in a movie he had seen on the late show one night —*Murders in the Rue Morgue* starring Bela Lugosi.

Just then the tall, thin man reached into the darkness of the wagon and brought out three western-style rifles that looked like Daisy BB guns. Billy felt a thump of excitement in his chest.

"Hey, what you got there anyway? Looks like a shootin' gallery!"

Magister nodded as he carefully arranged the three rifles along the countertop. "Yes, it is certainly that. It will be whatever you wish it to be."

Stepping closer still, Billy fought off the funny feelings at the bottom of his stomach. There was something strange going on, but he couldn't quite put his finger on it. He remembered what his father always told him about talking to strangers, but he was determined to get a closer look at those guns. Staring at the closest one, Billy admired the polished stock and its fine, tight grain. All the metal parts were smooth and bright, shining in the dim light, soaking up the evening in their blue-black depths. Billy had never seen such a finely crafted rifle. They couldn't be *real* guns, but they sure didn't look like any BB guns he'd ever seen. Absently he stared up into the gallery itself—and stepped back involuntarily.

It was so black inside the wagon, so totally *empty*, that Billy was startled by its sight. For a moment, he felt a wave of nausea clutch at him, like the dizzying sensation of suddenly standing on the edge of the deepest, darkest pit ever imagined. There was no end to the black depths, no end to the wagon itself. He kept telling himself that nothing could be so godawful dark. It was like something that soaked up light like a sponge, like the wagon had no insides. That last thought hung in his mind, scaring him with its possibilities. He wanted to turn away from the darkness, but there was some secret part of him that could have let him stare into the gallery indefinitely.

At last Billy turned away, looking at Magister. "Boy, that's really something! Where you from, anyway?"

"Many places," said Magister as he walked toward the front of the wagon.

Billy followed for several steps, again looking at the lettering on the side panel. "I guess that's you, huh? Mister Magister?"

"Yes, I am Magister."

"How come you're dressed up like that? You some kind of magician?"

Magister paused, shook his head slowly. "No, there is no magic here."

Billy watched him for a moment, waiting to see if the man had anything further to add. When he turned away, making an adjustment to the front of the wagon, Billy cleared his throat again.

"Well, you sure got a nice-lookin' setup, mister. You wouldn't mind if when I got to town, I told some of the folks you're out here, would you?"

"Not at all. Do as you wish." The man's cape fluttered gracefully as he turned to face the boy.

Billy stepped back a bit, then turned and walked quickly to his bike, throwing up the kickstand and jumping on.

"Okay, mister . . . thanks! See you later!"

The man made no reply as Billy pedaled off, reaching the outskirts of Brampton within a minute. He glided past Wiggins' Texaco, the plumbing supply house, and into the midst of the two-story row of shops and storefronts. When he reached the corner of Center and Madison, the sight of Strong's Grocery reminded him that he was supposed to bring home butter for his mom. Billy pulled up to the sidewalk and went in.

He always liked the smell in Mr. Strong's store. The mixture of spices and nuts, of freshly ground coffee and moist greens, all blended together to make a pleasant atmosphere. Mr. Strong was standing behind the counter, as usual, reading the *Des Moines Register*. He looked up at Billy through his steel-frame glasses and smiled.

"Hello, Billy. What can I do for you?"

Billy mentioned the butter for his mom and walked to the cold-cabinet at the rear of the store. Tilden Strong nodded and returned to his newspaper. A thin, refined-looking man with graying, thinning hair, and a carefully trimmed Errol Flynn mustache, he was a soft-spoken man, with a kindly face to which smiles came easily. He always wore white shirts and regimental-striped ties with colors that coordinated with his button-down-the-front sweaters. Strong wore these clothes season after season and always looked neat and comfortable, regardless of the weather.

"Hey, Mr. Strong," said Billy as he hefted the butter to the counter. "You hear about that carnival man yet?"

"Here's your change, Billy," said Tilden Strong as he rang up the amount on his old black cash register. "*What* carnival man?"

"I just seen him outside of town. Settin' up his wagon on the meadow. He's got a real neat shootin' gallery! You oughta go out and take a look at it!"

Strong smiled as he put the butter in a brown bag, shaking his head. "No, Billy. I'm afraid I'm getting too old for that sort of thing." Then, as he looked at Billy's shining face, he realized that his words had come almost automatically, that he was speaking from expectation rather than conviction. You should never be too old to have fun, he thought quickly.

Billy grabbed up the bag and headed for the door. "Well, see you later," he said.

"You know, Billy . . . maybe you're right. Maybe I *should* go down and take a look at that gallery."

The boy grinned. "Hey, that's neat. I'm going to tell everybody about it! Bye—and thanks!"

At just about the same time, down at Wiggins' Texaco, Sam Havens, chief gas jockey and day man at the station, was seated in the "office," clock-watching toward six, when he would be getting off. It always seemed to Sam that the last hour of the workday was twice as long as any of the others. He just couldn't figure it out, even though he thought about it quite a bit. There were lots of things he'd sit and think about, and never figure them out, and then he'd be pissed at himself for wasting time on it. Some things he could figure, but that damned clock thing really got to him.

Sam was just under five feet eight inches in his work boots, but a couple of inches taller when he was getting dressed up to go out somewhere, on account of those elevator shoes he got from the mail-order place last spring. They were brown wing tips, which he didn't care for too much, but they sure did make him taller. He had a lumpy, doughy face, even though he was built wiry like a weasel, and his chin just kind of faded away into his neck where his Adam's apple stuck out like a knot on a tree. His eyes were small and widely set, and Sam thought that was why his nose looked big. Optical delusion, he called it. His oily hair was thinning out on top, and the thought of going bald bothered him to no end. At least he could be thankful for his personality. He always kept the boys down at Donnegan's laughing, and that made him feel real good inside. Yeah, he thought as he watched that clock, I oughta be thankful. Yessireebob.

A bell rang in the station and Sam was yanked from his thoughts. It was caused by a car running over those new rubber hoses that the boss had picked up from the salesman out of Chicago. The hoses had only been out there since July, and Sam Havens hated them already. It used to be much better when he could just saunter out to the pumps real easylike. A lot of the drivers would go into a slow burn, but Sam could always say that he hadn't seen them pull up. Now, with them hoses, there'd be no more of that kind of thing. Course, there was talk of Wiggins going self-service.

Outside, an old, boxy '79 Chevy sat by the pumps. Sam recognized it as Doc Finlay's, probably coming back from some house calls.

"How ya doin', Doc?" he said, approaching the car. "Lose anybody today!?"

Sam laughed at his own joke while Finlay simply frowned. "Fill it up, will you, please, Sam?"

"Gotcha, Doc. How 'bout the oil? That okay?"

Finlay nodded as Sam rattled the nozzle off the pump and into the car's tank. He leaned on the windowsill and smiled at Homer Finlay, knowing that his jokes really got to the old man. "So what's new, Doc?"

The doctor looked at him for a moment before answering, as though wondering if Sam was serious or not. "Not much," he said finally. "See the new carnival man yet?"

"What carnival man?" A light sparked in Sam's eyes.

"Out off Center Street, right outside of town."

"Another carnival comin' in . . . this late? No kiddin'?"

"Nope. Didn't say a *whole* carnival. Just one man and a wagon . . . and a *horse,* if you can believe it. Saw him while I was driving in. Looks like he's fixing to set up a shooting gallery."

The automatic shutoff clicked, and Sam Havens pumped in enough gas to round out the price, then pulled the nozzle from the tank. "That's seventeen bucks, Doc. A shootin' gallery, huh?"

Doc Finlay handed him a twenty and shrugged. "Don't know more than that. Just saw him on the way in, that's all. You want to know about it so bad, just take a walk down and see."

Sam nodded as he pulled out a thick wad of bills from his coveralls, brandishing it like he was a big Texas spender. One of his little fantasies was that all that gas money was his, and he liked to flash it around like he figured the rich guys did. He peeled off the change with a flourish.

Doc Finlay drove off, and Sam ambled back to the station, thinking about that carnival attraction. He had been planning to stop off at Donnegan's on the way home, but now he didn't much feel like it. Not so early on, at least. Maybe that shootin' gallery would be just the ticket. Yessireebob. The clock on the wall read 5:56. The boss would be rolling in pretty soon. Sam smiled. Perfect timing, it was. Sam always did figure himself to be a good shot, and maybe now he'd have a chance to prove it to some of the boys.

A dull red pickup rumbled up to the side lot just then, and Phil Wiggins got out and entered the office.

"Hiya, Chief!" said Sam, fumbling a Marlboro out of his pack, lighting up. "Ya get that one, Phil? You know, Texaco? Boss? Chief?" Havens laughed before taking a drag.

Old Phil Wiggins just shook his head and held out his hand. Sam gave him the wad of bills. "Here ya go, boss. Johannsen finished up at four. I'm headin' out to see that carnival man."

Wiggins nodded. "Yep, I wish I could join you. I just heard some of the fellas talkin' about it up at Donnegan's. Looks like you might have a little company, Sam."

"Yeah, well, if they do, they're gonna see *some* shootin'! See you later, Phil."

Havens gave his Texaco cap a jaunty little tug, the way he'd seen Tyrone Power adjust his flying helmet in one of those World War II movies once, and walked out of the office. The day had cooled down considerably, and now the temperature was just right. Shootin' weather, thought Sam, laughing to himself. Still a couple hours before dark, and plenty of time to have a little fun. It was about time something different came to Brampton. Yessiree-bob.

CHAPTER 4

Clarence Williams walked happily down Center Street till he came to the Ford dealership on the corner of Grover's Road, where he turned left toward home. He was a spindly black boy of eleven with an easy bounce in his step. His face was long, dominated by large brown eyes and a bright, gap-toothed smile. He always wore his big brother's old clothes, and the sizes never seemed to be the right ones, but he still managed to look, in his mama's words, "right presentable."

Clarence was feeling pleased with himself, having collected his wages for his Saturday work. His right pocket was filled as he walked along: $2.50 for sweeping out the back stairs at Brampton Pharmacy; $2.00 for delivering groceries to Widow Shelton, plus a fifty-cent tip; and another $4.50 for stuffing mailing envelopes about the big sale at Mr. Hannah's dry goods store. That was practically ten dollars. It had been a good day. He figured that his mama would probably want some of it, not for herself, but to save in the Nestle's Quik tin she kept in the cupboard over the sink. She was saving money for Clarence, for what she called "your college."

He didn't really mind that she always did that, but he knew he didn't have any college, and wasn't so sure he wanted to go to anybody else's. He was pretty sure you didn't have to go to that much school to be a train engineer, and that's what he wanted to do more than anything in the whole world. Even if it was just for Amtrak.

But that didn't really matter, he figured. Even if mama took five dollars, he would still have enough to go to the movies at the Imperial. The marquee out front and the posters said they were having a big double-feature matinee next Saturday: *The Thing with the Knife* and *He Knows When You're Asleep*. Except Clarence wasn't sure he liked those scary movies much, on account of the bad case of the frights he would get trying to go to sleep after seeing them. They were fun while you were watching them, but later on . . . *that's* when things got bad.

But for three dollars it was worth a few frights, especially a double feature. Clarence smiled to himself as he walked along. He passed Nelson's Field where some of the white kids were playing ball, and down Grover's Road past the mulberry bushes and the occasional tree, until he came to the railroad tracks and the little road which snaked off to the Brampton Depot.

He crossed the tracks and ambled along the roadbed, stepping on the ties, up to where the depot sat empty and baking in the quiet sun. The building was always deserted on the weekends, and Clarence liked to come up there and think about things. The depot, now withered and old, used to be a regular stop on the Rock Island Line for the old *Crescent Limited*, which ran from Omaha through Des Moines and Cedar Rapids, up to Dubuque, and on in to Chicago. Just thinking of that big, gleaming locomotive gliding through the cornfields made Clarence smile.

Reaching the depot, Clarence climbed up to the platform, where the gray paint was peeling off the wood in great arcing slabs. He stared off down the tracks to where they curved off to a tiny point, imagining a big train heading on down the line. Clarence didn't do too well in school, but he sure did know all there was to know about trains. He could tell you all the types of locomotives, weights, numbers of wheels, destinations, just about everything. And he hadn't read it in any books, either. Ever since he was a little boy, he had sat down with his daddy at night by a crackling fire and listened to that big, brown, bald-headed man talk trains. Coming down to the depot always reminded him of his daddy, and he guessed that was why he liked to go there so often.

His daddy had worked for the railroads, not as a trainman like Clarence was going to be, but just as a trackman. For almost twenty years his daddy rode handcars on the Rock Island, lugging ties, laying rail, driving home spikes. He did it right up until the day Clarence came home from school and found his mama crying in the kitchen, a pan of snap beans in her lap. That day, when Clarence was nine years old, she told him his daddy wouldn't be coming home no more. Not ever again.

He had cried a long time when he heard that, and tears still tried to leak out of the corners of his eyes when he thought about it. Looking down the tracks, first one way, then the other, Clarence knew that somewhere out there was where it had happened. A caboose had broken loose from its coupling on a siding and had rolled down a long grade, silent as a cat, but fast as the rain, until it came up on a crew replacing bolts on a spur-line switch. His mama never did tell him how his daddy died, but Clarence hung around the railroad men as much as he could, and pretty soon after that Bad Day, he heard a brakeman and a signalman talking about what had happened. They said that nigger never saw it comin', that it just knocked him down and cut him open like a split pea. And when it went on down the line, there were two halves of that nigger, one on each side of the rail.

Clarence drew in a deep breath, let it out real easy. It made him feel better when he thought about his daddy. He never had told his mama about that story. He knew he never would.

There was a breeze blowing up the tracks and it fluttered inside his baggy shirt. It felt good on his nut-brown skin, and he turned away from the platform, jumping back down to the road. Mama said that Big Cal (that's what she always called him) was up in Railroad Heaven now, and that he was waitin' —waitin' to see his young boy go to college. Clarence looked up at the fading blue sky and smiled. He wondered if that was true, and hoped that maybe Big Cal might rather be waitin' to see one of them monster diesels come highballin' through the depot with Clarence at the window. He sure hoped so.

He walked back to the crossing and down Grover's Road till he came to a row of slant-roofed houses.

There were nine houses on the road front, and seven more down the lane, all connected by a roughly paved street. Telephone poles stuck up between the yards, and bushes and broken picket fences separated the properties. Clarence came up to his own house, waving to his mama, who was hanging wash in the side yard. His sister, Merrilou, was playing in the tire swing off the big elm, and his mama was humming a gospel tune as she worked. It sure was a nice day, he thought.

CHAPTER 5

Six o'clock arrived in Brampton, and Tilden Strong went to the front door of his grocery to hang up the CLOSED sign. He pulled down the shades and returned to the register to count out the day's receipts. He entered his figures in his ledger carefully, making each number neat and even, bound up the bills in paper wrappers, and put everything in a canvas bag for a Monday morning deposit at the Farmer's Bank. He had told Joanna that he was going to inventory the canned goods before coming home to dinner, but now he was thinking that the extra work would certainly keep until Monday, which was always a slow day. Yes, it would keep just fine.

Tilden Strong kept thinking about the Parkins boy and that smile which had illuminated his face. That, plus the mention of the carnival attraction, had touched Strong deeply. Down, into his heart of hearts, where the private, precious memories are kept, Tilden Strong felt a growing sadness. The times of his youth seemed so far away, almost forgotten, like old toys in an attic trunk. It occurred to Tilden that he was getting old very quickly. The silver in his hair, Nathaniel off to Cornell, Louisa entering her senior year of high school, the mortgage almost paid off . . . all the milestones being ticked off as he rambled along. There wasn't much left to get excited about anymore, and he envied the pure joy that he'd felt in Billy Parkins. The urge to reach back in time and grab some of that lost joy seemed suddenly overpowering.

Tilden checked the lock on the front door and went out the back to the alley where he kept his still-shining Toronado. He drove down to Church Lane, turned left, then another left on Center, toward the meadow.

Almost immediately he saw a small crowd gathered on the left side of the road. He felt foolish driving his car such a short distance, but he hadn't realized the wagon was so close to town. There was only one other automobile on the shoulder—a faded blue pickup which he did not recognize.

As he crunched across the gravel and shut off the ignition, several men in the crowd turned to take silent notice. There were no more than ten men standing in front of a long black carnival wagon, all trumped up with decoration and gilded lettering. Some Magnificent Gallery, he thought sardonically, shaking his head. It didn't look like much of an attraction, and he reproached himself for listening to the hyperbole of a small boy before catching himself up short. Wait. Wasn't that what it was all about? Those excited feelings of a small boy . . . wasn't that why he was here?

Tilden Strong smiled, feeling like an old fuddy-duddy, and resolved to shake that self-image. He stepped from the car, crossed the road, and entered the meadow. Some of the men nodded, tipped their hats; others spoke curt greetings.

One of them, Joseph Dutton, approached him slowly, a sly grin working about the corners of his mouth. "Well, Mr. Tilden Strong, how are ya? Didn't expect to see you out here."

Dutton threw back his head and laughed. He wore a bloodstained white apron over jeans and a white shirt with rolled-up sleeves. He must have come directly from his work at the butcher shop. He was a large man with a round face that was so fleshy he always appeared to be squinting. Balding, pug-nosed, and thick-lipped, Dutton was an unconscious caricature of the animal which produced at least half of his meats. He was an unattractive man with a personality to match his looks.

"I'm afraid I don't understand," said Tilden, fighting the feeling that he was being intimidated by the large man.

"I don't know—shootin' gallery doesn't seem like your cup of tea, know what I mean?" Dutton looked for approval in the townspeople around him. Several grinned and nodded their heads, which seemed to please Joseph Dutton.

Tilden tried to ignore the remark, but found himself responding in a soft voice. "I don't know, Joseph. It's been such a long time since I've tried anything like this. I thought it might be fun."

He turned from the butcher and the others to look at the gallery. There were three people at the counter, all shouldering rifles, popping away at the darkness: one of the Whitaker boys; Tim Hargrove, who worked the Bester farm; and Sam Havens, that grinning fool from the Texaco station. Off to the right, standing near the front of the wagon and partially obscured by the evening shadows, stood a man in black. A cape and a droopy, broad-brimmed hat concealed his frame and features. The man watched the crowd dispassionately.

"I suppose that's Mister Magister?" asked Strong.

"Yeah," said Dutton. "He's really somethin', ain't he? Weirdest-lookin' fella I've seen in a while."

Strong nodded. "Yes, he's quite theatrical."

Dutton laughed. "Whatever that means! Sometimes you really crack me up with those fancy words, Tilden. Whatever you say . . ."

The men who had been listening to their conversation lost interest, and turned to watch the gallery. Tilden used the opportunity to steer Dutton away from his initial aggressive remarks.

"What's the cost?" he asked casually.

Dutton chuckled. "That's the damnedest part of it. The man says it's only a quarter! Can you believe that?"

"A quarter? That *is* cheap, isn't it?"

Dutton stepped closer, leaning in conspiratorially. "And get this"—he nudged Strong with his elbow —"that's a quarter for all the shots you want."

"As many as you want? No limit?" Strong was truly surprised.

"Yep. They say you just keep shootin's till you knock everything down. I never heard of that kind of deal before, but it sounds like a real bargain to me." Dutton hooked his fat, sausagelike thumbs into the strings of his apron and rocked absently back and forth. He looked more like a cartoon character than a real person.

"Yes, it certainly is," said Tilden, looking back to the wagon.

At that same moment, Sam Havens lay his gun on

the counter, turned around, and mopped his oily forehead with a kerchief. He let out a long breath and walked over to Dutton and Strong. His place at the gallery was immediately taken by someone in the crowd.

"Hello, Sam," said Dutton. "Well, you think it's worth a quarter?"

"Hey, that thing's really somethin'!" Havens grinned, breaking into a childish smile. Tilden noticed the brown stains on his teeth and shuddered inwardly. "You boys goin' to give it a try?"

"Hell, yeah! We came all the way out here, didn't we?" Dutton laughed and slapped Havens on the shoulder, who grinned appreciatively like a dog receiving a rub on the head from his master.

"It's a funny thing, though," said Havens, jerking a thumb back toward the wagon. "Never seen no gallery like that before . . ." What passed for pensiveness in Sam Havens briefly flashed on his face, and Tilden Strong picked up on it.

"What do you mean, Sam?"

"Well . . . I'm not rightly certain, Mr. Strong. It's them targets, I guess. Queerest-lookin' things I ever saw."

"Sam, what're you talking about? Get to the point, will you?" Dutton's demeanor changed instantly from jovial chuckler to a prosecuting attorney. That was his way, thought Strong. Lull you into the garden, then pounce on you for all it was worth. He was a school-yard bully who had never grown up.

Havens looked up quickly, obviously respecting the butcher. "Well, let me explain. Like I was sayin', them targets are kinda funny. Strange. No ducks or bull's-eyes, no dancin' Indians, nothing like that. Just a buncha funny-looking faces . . ."

"What?" asked Strong.

"Buncha faces," said Havens. "Hard to describe 'em, really. They just kinda float in the darkness, glowin' like Halloween masks, you know? Hell of a thing . . ." He pulled a Marlboro from a pack, fired it up with his Bic, took a drag, and drew in the smoke through clenched teeth. Then he shrugged and looked out at the crowd. "Looks like it's goin' to get half the town out here, though, don't it?"

"Well, why not?" said Dutton. "Summer's done in. Folks don't want to see it go. They're all out here tryin' to pick up one last piece of summertime."

Tilden Strong looked back at the wagon, which seemed to grow larger and somehow more ominous in the fading light. He glanced at the man called Magister, and had the odd sensation that the man's shadowed, hidden eyes were looking directly at him. It was an unsettling feeling, and Strong loosened his tie, clearing his throat nervously, looking away quickly.

"You know, I was just thinking," he said to Dutton softly. "Don't you think it's a bit odd?"

"What's that?"

"Well, just this one man, traveling alone, so late in the season?"

Joseph Dutton harrumphed loudly. "Ah, who cares about that? He's just a carnival man, that's all. His business is *his* business. He probably got cut off from the rest of his bunch, or maybe he's fixin' to join up with some outfit south of here? Who cares? It's not important, anyway."

Sam Havens listened to Dutton with rapt attention, nodding his head for silent emphasis. Tilden decided that he was probably being overly melodramatic, that there was most likely nothing to really wonder about. It was time to loosen up, to stop worrying all the time, and simply have some fun.

"Yes, you're probably right, Joseph," he said. "It's not important as long as we have a good time . . ."

Dutton chuckled, pleased that his oration had been so convincing. "Yeah, so why're we standin' way back here? Let's get up a little closer so we can have a crack at it. Sam, you hold back awhile since you already had a turn."

Havens flipped his cigarette onto the shoulder and stuffed his hands into his overalls. When he did that, his shoulders slumped, and with his wooden, rough-hewn features, to Strong he resembled nothing more than a ventriloquist's dummy.

The three men walked closer to the wagon, where the others waited their turn, passing time in idle chatter. Doc Ames, the veterinarian, was there, and Tilden also recognized the bank's vice-president, Mr. Winslow, and Doc Burroughs, the pharmacist. It seemed like everyone in Brampton, regardless of social standing, did not mind coming out to the meadow and rubbing elbows with each other, waiting for a chance to try out a small carnival attraction. Tilden attributed it to the routine of small-town life, and the need for something new, anything new, which might provide a respite, and perhaps some genuine entertainment. The shopkeepers talked business, the farmers discussed the weather, and the working folk speculated on the coming World Series. Everyone seemed to be having a grand time.

Someone tapped Dutton on the shoulder, and Tilden took the opportunity to drift away into the crowd, closer to the gallery. People greeted him casually but not with what could be called real friendliness. Most knew him because they frequented his grocery, but not one *really* knew him. When they saw him, they saw Mr. Strong the grocer, not Tilden Strong the person.

For some reason, he looked up at Magister, and again, it seemed that the man in black was staring straight at him. It had to be some kind of illusion, he thought abashedly. Something about the way the shadows from his hat fell across his eyes—maybe that was it. Add to that a good dose of natural paranoia, and Tilden had a good rationalization, a reason not to think about it seriously.

Am I really paranoid? he thought. Perhaps not. It was no secret that he was not the most well liked man in Brampton. He was respected, to be sure, but not liked, included, invited. And in a town like Brampton there was a big difference between the two. He did not know why it was the case, but after almost twenty-two years in the town, he was certain that it was true. Maybe it was because he was not an Iowa native; he'd been born in New Jersey and hadn't come to Brampton until he was in his midtwenties. Marrying a local girl didn't seem to matter. Or perhaps it was his college education and his extensive vocabulary. He did not really know, and thinking about it only served to heighten the feelings of solitude. He was probably making things worse than they actually were.

He shook his head and moved through the small crowd, unable to shake the impression that Magister was still watching him. He thought about the carnival man's name, Magister, and wondered if it had any relationship to the Latin word from which it might have derived. But he put it quickly out of mind, along with the idea that he might discuss it with any of the others. They would not know what he was talking about, and would put it down as Tilden Strong trying to show off how much he knew about words and things like that.

Turning to the wagon, he saw that Bill Holbrook, the salesman for John Deere, had just completed his turn at the gallery. No one else was close enough to fill his place, and there did not appear to be a line, so Tilden edged up to the counter, placed a quarter in the Mason jar to one side, and reached for a rifle. *Carpe diem*, he thought with a grin.

The other two men at the counter paid him no attention as he picked up the gun and hefted it for a moment in his hands, getting its feel, thinking that it was quite heavy for a carnival prop. It did not resemble any carnival gun he had ever seen. It looked bright and polished and new, its metal parts obviously tooled with care and craft. He had not handled a real rifle since his basic training at Fort Dix, but he still recalled how one felt in a man's hands.

But he pushed the thought from his mind. This could not be a real gun, and he was still being a suspicious, old man. Let go, he thought. Loosen up, and enjoy. He grinned self-consciously and stared into the gallery. Into a darkness never before imagined. It was a special kind of darkness, so total that he felt he could reach out and touch it. A complete absence of light. A paradox which his mind could not accept as easily as his eyes. And then, illuminated by an unseen source, the targets began to appear. They floated effortlessly, some close, and others far away, very far away. It seemed as though the distance between the targets and the counter was far greater than the mere length of the wagon. It was impossible, but it was a strikingly effective optical trick. Tilden Strong had the feeling of staring into an emptiness without limit, and he became transfixed by the sensation as his mind wrestled with the image, trying to rationalize it. It was like peering out into the night sky where worlds hung magically distant yet brilliantly clear. It was a dizzying, almost hypnotic effect.

He blinked and drew a breath, to break the spell. Raising the rifle slowly, he brought it to firing position and aimed down its sight. The targets floated in front of him and he remembered Sam Havens' lack of ability to describe them. Faces, Havens said, but odd, different. How odd? How different?

Faces.

Bizarre caricatures of human countenances. Exaggerated features. Long lantern jaws, sunken cheeks, deep-socketed eyes, bulging fish eyes, beetle brows. Round faces, puffy-cheeked and bloated. They were the faces of night, of dreams, broken and twisted. The faces of back alleys and old houses, of dim fears and strange joys. They flickered and bobbed, glowing eerily in the void of the gallery.

Tilden exhaled as he sighted one of the closer targets and squeezed the trigger slowly, as he had been taught on a dusty firing range so long ago. When the trigger clicked, he tensed, expecting a recoil, a report, but there was none. Instead, he heard a soft hissing sound and saw a change in the illumination of the target he had hit. For an instant, it grew brighter, then changed from pale yellow to a bright crimson, before winking out. He felt a small rush of elation as he achieved the small success, not expecting such accuracy on the first shot. Flushed with sudden confidence, he aimed at another target, paused carefully to center it in his sights, and squeezed the trigger. Again the flaring of the light, the fade to scarlet, and oblivion. Tilden Strong felt boyhood excitement flood into him. This was fun. He aimed at another face, and then another, and kept firing at the faces which floated in the blackness, faces that disappeared under the constant rain of fire. He became entranced by the balletic movements of the targets, by the unconsciously choreographed movements of firing, flaring, vanishing, and the turretlike glide of the rifle to begin the sequence anew. He lost all touch with the world of the meadow and the talking crowds and the shooter at his left elbow. Everything narrowed and fell into the black well of the gallery and its floating faces. He immersed himself in the mechanical, yet somehow organic, act of sighting, firing, gliding the sight to a new face, and the burst of pleasure as yet another winked out.

There was no sense of time passing, and he did not know how long he had been shooting, but suddenly he realized that he had destroyed them all, that there were no new targets appearing. He had gotten them all, he thought, and felt the pleasure of a job well done. Tilden Strong felt sated, appeased, and he lay down the rifle with no regrets. It was a sensation of completeness, of true satisfaction. He felt just fine.

Someone shouldered past him, taking his place at the counter, and he noticed how much larger the crowd had become. Word of mouth was a powerful agent in a small town, and it did not take long to exercise its power. More than thirty people milled about the area as though they were attending a church social.

"Well, how'd you like it?" asked a familiar voice. Pudgy fingers were rudely jabbing at the back of his shoulder.

Tilden turned to see Joseph Dutton looking down at him. "It was . . . incredible," he said. "Really fine, Mr. Dutton. I don't remember when I've had so much fun."

"Yep, that's what everybody's sayin'," said Dutton. "I guess I better get up there and get me a turn before it gets too dark. Millie'll already be wondering where I been."

Dutton slapped him roughly on the shoulder and turned toward the wagon. Tilden's eyes followed him for a moment, then his gaze was arrested by the silent figure of Magister, still shrouded by the lengthening shadows of the wagon. What an odd man he was, thought Tilden. So quiet and detached. Actually, it was quite a refreshing change from the usual barker's spiel—but it seemed in some way unnatural.

Tilden had a vague impression of something unsettling, not right. He struggled to bring it forth, to give it substance, but it would not come. Yet he knew there was something in his subconscious, on the brink of breaking through. But either it was in fact unimportant, or he did not want to confront it. Either way, it would not come to him. He shook his head, refocusing his vision, and hoped that no one had noticed his brief loss of touch with reality. All they had to do was see Tilden Strong staring off into space like a village idiot . . .

He checked his watch and saw that it was fast approaching eight o'clock. Time for him to be getting home, inventory or no. He crossed the street, where several other cars and pickups were now lined up with his Toronado. He started the ignition, put it in gear, and turned around toward Brampton. As he headed into town, he saw still more people walking out to the meadow. It was surprising how a single carnival wagon could have so much attraction to everyone.

Smiling, he drove along the deserted Center Street, past the square, down two blocks, to the familiar right turn on Jefferson, and another two blocks along a tree-shaded lane where his white, two-story bungalow huddled in a mass of shrubbery. It had been good to get out of the store and spend some time in the cool evening air, to have finally let go and simply enjoyed himself. But there was still that nagging impression that there had been something strange going on, something that he should have noticed.

As he pulled into the driveway and got out of the car, his feelings of unease increased. Something was, if not wrong, at least odd, about what he had done, had seen, and he wished he could articulate it.

He entered the house through the front door and was met by the sound of the television. Louisa sat in the far corner of the living room, watching Dan Ackroyd on some talk show. Ackroyd's comedy had never appealed to Tilden.

"Hello, Father," mumbled his daughter.

"Good evening, Lou. Where's your mother?"

She retained her zombielike expression for a moment, then looked up with a start. "Oh, what? She's in the kitchen, I guess . . ."

As she looked back to the screen, Tilden thought about the ambiguous nature of television. He was old enough to remember what it was like before everyone started buying them. Now lots of people often wondered what they did before the sets were invented. They talked more to one another, thought Tilden. At least that was one good thing about that shooting gallery—people were out socializing again.

One good thing? Now, why, he asked himself, had he thought about it like that?

He stood motionless in the foyer, feeling more distinctly that something was wrong.

And he remembered what it was.

The faces burst in his mind's eye like fireworks. It was something about the faces in the gallery. One of them, for the briefest instant, while it flickered and changed in the darkness, had seemed familiar.

It was odd that he had not realized it while he was standing at the counter, holding that gun in his hand. It was a subliminal perception—something seen by the eye, registered and imprinted upon the cortical receiving centers, but not consciously recognized at the moment of perception. Tilden had read an article about it once, which explained the technique in terms of advertising strategy. It told how viewers of movies and television were subjected to milli-second flashes of messages like "Have a Coke" or "Buy a Plymouth" without realizing it. Only later would they have a vague feeling, perhaps a craving for a Coca-Cola or an untraceable urge to see what the new car models might be like to drive.

Tilden shook his head. It could not be possible, and was most likely his imagination. But then, *maybe* it had been more than that.

The thought rebounded in his mind as he pushed through the kitchen door, where he saw his wife at the sink, washing dishes. Joanna was a short, thin woman who was not flattered by the styles currently in fashion. Her face was long, made longer by her pointed chin. She wore no lipstick, which made her mouth colorless and practically invisible, certainly nonsensual. Lines of age cut into her face so that she looked perpetually troubled and ill at ease. She looked up at him with steel-gray eyes which matched the streaks in her once-dark hair.

"Did you have trouble with that inventory? It's after eight," she said, turning back to her dishes.

Tilden walked to the kitchen table and sat down. He had thought of kissing her, but was afraid of how she might have reacted. But that wasn't what he was really thinking about. He struggled to find the correct way to tell her about the gallery, and what he thought he might have seen there. What he *did* see there.

"Til . . . I said it's after eight, what's kept you?" She did not turn around as she spoke—a habit which had begun to annoy him, although he had not mentioned it to her.

"Sorry, dear, I was thinking about something. I . . . I didn't do the inventory tonight." There, he thought. I've said it.

His wife turned around, wiping her hands on a tea towel. "What? Then where've you been? Louisa and I couldn't wait, so we've already had supper. I put yours in the fridge, but I'll have to heat it up. Where were you if you weren't at the store?"

Tilden stared at her for a moment before answering. He was remembering how beautiful she had looked to him when they first met at a dance at Rutgers. It was hard to believe that that young girl was the same woman glaring at him in the cold fluorescent light of the kitchen. Tilden hated fluorescent light because it made people look so unnaturally cold—an aspect of which Joanna had no additional need.

"A lot of people in town went out to the meadow," he said softly. "They went out to see this new carnival wagon that just came in." He paused. "Is there any coffee left in the pot?"

"A carnival wagon? Well, what were *you* doing there? A man of your age!" She took a cup and saucer from the cabinet and poured some coffee, placed it on the table in front of him.

"What do you mean by that—'a man of your age'? There were plenty of men out there older than me. I was just curious, that's all." He sipped from the cup, and the vapor steamed his glasses. He took them off and cleared them with a napkin. He continued to wipe them after they were clean—a nervous habit he had acquired sometime after Joanna had plagued him to give up his pipe.

"Well, what did they have in this 'wagon'? A bunch of naked dancing girls?"

"Come on, Jo . . . it wasn't anything like that. It was a shooting gallery."

Joanna laughed. It was a tinkling, high-pitched laugh, which sounded mockingly artificial. "Til, sometimes you really surprise me. A grown man going to a shooting gallery . . ."

"I wasn't alone. There were plenty of people out there, and it was fun," he said, thinking for a moment about the Williams boy and wondering if he was being totally honest with himself.

Joanna turned back to her dishes, drying them

with the tea towel and putting them away in the cabinet. "I'm sure it was great fun . . ."

"It was more than that, actually. I . . . wanted to . . . to talk to you about it." He blurted out the words and somehow they seemed inappropriate, awkward.

Joanna opened the Frigidaire and brought out a casserole dish, placing it in the oven. Turning, she looked at him as if he were a small boy. "Tilden, what makes you think I would be interested in such a thing?" She smirked to herself and continued putting away the dishes.

He wanted to say something, to get up and grab her by the shoulders and shake some sense into her. He wanted to tell her that she should be interested in what he had to say because *he* was interested in it. That should be reason enough.

But he said nothing, instead fighting the knot of tension which was building in his stomach.

"I'm sorry, Joanna," he finally said. "It's just that we never seem to talk to each other anymore."

"Well, we're both busy, you know," she said, not turning around.

He sipped his coffee, and tried to find the words to explain what it was that was bothering him. How could he possibly describe to her the oddness of that gallery? The emptiness of the wagon and the weird targets, the faces? And the one face in particular . . . To do it convincingly, he would have to speak carefully and without any sign that it was upsetting to him. He doubted if Joanna would have the patience for such a thing, or whether he would have the ability to convey to her how serious it was to him.

Tilden Strong sat in the cold light of the kitchen,

feeling terribly alone and helpless. He was becoming trapped in something which he did not understand, and he wanted to reach out to his wife, but was unable to make the first contact. His adventure had seemed so innocent, and now, in his mind at least, it had taken a dark turn, changing into something twisted. The more he thought about it, the more he knew that he could not explain it to her. To hear her mocking peal of laughter would crush him, and he could not bear that.

His wife placed a slightly warm plate of reheated roast beef and greasy potatoes in front of him. He was not hungry, but he began to eat mechanically. It was as though he were suddenly disconnected from everything that was familiar to him. All the things that had been so important to him were slowly drifting away, isolating him in a wasteland of confusion. Nathaniel was away at college and probably would not be returning; Louisa lived in a swirl of proms, rock-and-roll music, and television; Joanna was rushing headlong into a vicious, resentful menopause.

Looking up at her, he saw that she was smirking at him, shaking her head as though regarding the actions of an infant, or worse, the dodderings of a senile old man.

He hated himself for being unable to express his feelings, to explain what he was thinking. He felt terribly alone, abandoned with a frightful knowledge of something that he could not completely understand.

What am I going to do? he thought helplessly.

CHAPTER 6

Morning sunlight danced at Stella's windowsill, accompanied by a robin's song. She awoke slowly, with a fluttering of lashes, stretching, remembering the previous evening with a secret smile. *The Facts of Life and Love* had been restored to its place under her sweaters, and she was safe, she thought, then laughed silently to herself as she sat up. She did not want to fall prey to the taboos that Laura Gleesinger wrote about. She wanted to break out of the mold of thinking which had led people in the past to cover piano legs because they too much resembled a woman's calf. Even in Brampton today, there were people who felt it was unwise for a pregnant woman to be seen in public.

Her Aunt Leah was not that extreme, but Stella knew that it would be next to impossible to share her recent feelings with the older woman. It would simply have to be that way, she thought, as she climbed from beneath the covers and went across the hall to wash her face. The smell of bacon frying in the kitchen wafted up the stairs, and Stella was immediately hungry. Aunt Leah would be in a rush to have breakfast so that they would not be late for church, and Stella wished that they didn't have to go *every* Sunday.

She dressed quickly in yellow overalls and a ruffle-collared white blouse. As she put on her dressy shoes, she noticed how the elevated heel emphasized the curve of her calf. She liked the way it looked, and as she brushed out her hair in the mirror, she was pleased with the way it seemed to grab the sunlight and hold it in fluffy brightness. She wondered how she would look in a little mascara.

"Stella . . . Stella, you up yet?" Aunt Leah's voice floated up the stairs like the lilting notes of a piccolo.

"Yes, Auntie. I'm almost ready!"

"Hurry up, now. I've got breakfast on the table and it's after eight."

"Be down in a second," she said, thinking of eating and then walking up to Saint Matthew's. It wasn't that she didn't like to go to church; it was more that she was growing tired of the repetition. The gospels and the sermons were starting to all sound alike, and she was having more and more trouble making them have any relevance to the new thoughts and feelings she was beginning to have.

Perhaps she would see Jamie there. That was one consolation. Three weeks ago, her aunt had unwittingly led them into the same pew where Jamie and his parents were sitting, and they had sat right next to each other. The hour had passed so quickly—they had spent most of it stealing glances at one another, sharing secret smiles, and feeling a touch of electricity when they would accidentally touch hands or arms while standing or kneeling.

After breakfast, Stella and her aunt walked down

Church Lane and entered the white clapboard building. They sat in one of the pews closest to the altar; Stella was afraid to turn around to see if Jamie was there. Her thoughts were turned inward and she had no recollection of Father Doheny's sermon. Suddenly, it seemed, the service was over and everyone was filing out, where they would mingle and gossip for a few minutes before returning home. Stella stood with Aunt Leah on the front lawn, watching for Jamie, only half paying attention to the conversations around her. But she could not help but notice that almost everyone was talking about some carnival wagon that had just come to town.

She picked up snippets of the discussions, and her interest picked up. A dark man. A funny wagon with weird targets. A shooting gallery. A stranger outside of town. Carnival wagon without any carnival. A man in black. Mister Magister. Hell of a good time. A dark man.

Everyone, it seemed, was talking about it. Excited whispers and hushed tones. It was as though the congregation felt it might be wrong to be talking about a tawdry amusement on a Sunday morning. Or was it more than that?

Well, whatever it was, Jamie would probably know about it. She hoped that he had come to the nine o'clock service. Then she saw him, coming out of the double front doors, his parents behind him. Rushing up, she smiled and stood before him.

"Good morning, Jamie." She hoped he liked her in her fancy clothes, her brushed-out hair.

"Hi, Stella. How are you? Did you get to the library yesterday? Sorry I couldn't make it. I had to help my dad with the lawn."

"That's all right," she said brightly, genuinely

happy to see him. "Why don't we have a picnic, down by the mill? I can make a lunch when I get home."

Jamie ran a hand through his rumpled hair, looked nervously at his parents, who were waiting for him a respectful distance away. "Sure! That sounds great, Stella. I'll come by in about an hour or so, okay?"

"That'll be fine."

"See you then! Gotta go now. Bye." He turned and joined his parents, walking to the parking lot in the back. Stella watched them leave, noticing how ruggedly handsome Jamie's father was, and how his son was starting to resemble him.

It was almost two hours before Jamie knocked on the front door. Which was fine, because Stella was in the kitchen just finishing mixing up some potato salad. The fried chicken was already wrapped in aluminum foil and packed in the basket. Aunt Leah, who had been in the living room listening to the radio, let him in, and Stella heard his voice offer a polite greeting and thanks. Stella could tell by the tone of her voice that her aunt approved of Jamie, and she was glad. While she finished the basket, Stella heard them talking about the weather, the coming of school, even a brief mention of the new carnival man.

Stella considered the notion she'd been harboring for the past hour or so, trying to decide yes or no. On impulse she ran up the back stairs and took her journal from her desk, brought it back down to the kitchen, and concealed it in the bottom of the picnic basket.

Jamie and Stella left the house and walked down Sycamore to Grover's Road, which led to the Wells

River Mill. There was little conversation as they made their way down the shaded street, due to nervousness. Aunt Leah had remarked that this was the first time a boy had called on her, and Stella thought about this as Jamie strolled by her side, lugging the wicker basket. The times she had met him at the library or the luncheonette were more casual, less formal, but now they were embarking on what was officially known as a "date."

Gingerbreaded houses with sweeping front porches and high-peaked roofs lined the street. Tall oaks and elms bent their boughs close to turrets and widows' walks. A breeze weaved through trellises choked with roses and snapdragons. People sat on their porches reading the Sunday papers, or trimmed their lawns with rattling mowers, or sculpted their hedges. It was a quiet, lazy afternoon in Brampton, everyone taking advantage of one of the last weekends of Indian summer.

When they reached Nelson's Field, they turned left on Grover's Road, passed the railroad tracks and the depot, and headed down the section of country road everybody called Mudville. A small stretch of broken-down houses huddled on the right side of the road. There was an ambulance from the Simpsonville Hospital parked in front of one house.

"Hey, look!" said Jamie. "I wonder what happened. There's Doc Finlay's car, too."

As they walked closer, they saw a small crowd, mostly black women in big, full dresses or jeans and bright blouses. A handful of children hung by their sides, all knees and elbows in their faded clothes. Some of the women were openly crying, and the children seemed confused.

Stella and Jamie stopped directly across from the

ambulance. A young, pudgy man in hospital whites leaned against the opened back door of the vehicle, smoking a cigarette.

"Let's see what's going on," said Jamie.

"No, maybe we better not . . ."

"Hey, it'll be okay. Come on."

They crossed the road and Jamie politely asked the ambulance attendant what was happening.

The man grinned and shook his head. He took a final drag on his cigarette and flipped it expertly into the road. "Ah, I don't know . . . " His voice was caustic with disinterest. "One of them women called up half-crazy. Somethin' wrong with one of her kids, said he was dyin' or somethin' . . ."

"Oh, no," said Stella, looking at the group of sobbing women.

"Ain't no big deal, the way I figure it," said the ambulance attendant, shaking another Camel from his pack, lighting it. "They all got so many, I don't suppose they'll miss one too bad." He laughed lightly, coughing on his cigarette smoke.

"Let's get out of here, Stella," said Jamie, touching her arm, looking embarrassed.

They turned to see Doc Finlay walking resolutely from the nearest run-down house, his white fedora hiding most of his down-turned face. He was wearing a light blue, rumpled seersucker suit, and carrying his battered black bag. He did not see Stella and Jamie until he was almost beside them.

"Dr. Finlay," said Jamie, "what happened in there?"

"Oh, hello, kids," he said, placing his bag on the front seat of his car, pausing to draw a breath and let it out with a sigh. "Don't rightly know, really. One of Mrs. Williams' boys, Clarence. He just fell over dead this morning. Right before noon."

"He's . . . dead?" asked Stella, her voice just above a whisper.

"Can't understand it," said Finlay. "Young healthy boy, too. Dead. Just like that. That poor woman—lost her husband a few years back, and now this. Don't make sense."

"I can't believe it," said Jamie. "Little Clarence . . . he used to work with me sometimes down at the hardware."

Doc Finlay shook his head slowly, adjusted his hat, and climbed into his car. "Well, there's no need for you children to hang around here. I'll be seeing you. Got some business to take care of down at the funeral home, looks like. Bye, now."

They said good-bye and crossed the road, neither able to speak for a moment.

"I wish there was something we could do," said Stella after they had walked a few feet. "I feel guilty almost, just walking off and having fun . . ."

Jamie stopped and looked at her intently. His brown eyes were deep and penetrating. He had never looked at her like that before. "Stella, I understand what you're feeling, I really do. But there isn't much we *can* do about it. Do you want to go back and see Ms. Williams?"

Stella shook her head. She didn't know the woman. She didn't know what she wanted. There was a lump growing in her throat and she was afraid that she might start to cry, afraid of what Jamie might think if she did.

"Hey, it's all right, Stella. It's okay to cry if you want to." Jamie put his hand on her shoulder and she could feel his firm touch, his warmth, and his strength.

"I don't want to cry. I just don't know what to feel. Oh, Jamie, I don't want you to see me like this."

Jamie smiled gently. "That's all right. Even if you did, you'd just be . . . being yourself. You'd be letting me know more about you, and that's a good thing."

He stared into her green eyes, and at that moment he seemed so grown-up and so strong. She knew that he understood. The tightening in her throat lessened, and she knew there would be no tears.

"Jamie, what should we do?"

"Do? There's nothing to do but keep on going. Life's for the living, that's what they say. And in this case, they're right. Let's go down to the mill and talk for a while."

Back around the turn of the century, the land which banked the Wells River and the floodplain beyond had been a fair-sized forest, and since lumber sources were not plentiful in Iowa, people had built a sawmill on the banks of the Wells. It had cut most of the planking and beams for nearly all of the houses in Brampton and other surrounding towns. As the years passed and the trees were thinned out, the sawmill went into a decline, and was finally shut down after World War II. The building remained, though soon nature reclaimed it with moss and ivies. Even though the county had condemned it, the building still hunkered down along the bank of the Wells, next to a stone-buttressed cataract which once powered the mill wheel.

It was a favorite picnic spot for campers and young people, and it was in the shadows of the mill that Stella and Jamie spread their tablecloth. Around them, the rush of the falls, the leaf-scramblings of small animals, and the natural symphony of bird-songs blended together, easing the tension of the previous hour.

After they had eaten, Stella felt better. It was good to be out in the fresh air, and she was glad that Jamie had convinced her to have the picnic after all. She seemed to draw strength from Jamie, who was so confident. He spoke with the sureness of someone older than his years, and he seemed to understand the world, how it worked and why. She was beginning to believe that she could trust him. He never laughed at her questions, and her emotional nature did not seem to bother him. Yes, Jamie might be the one with whom secret thoughts might be shared.

After they had talked for a while, she took her journal from the basket and asked him if she could read some of it to him. He nodded and lay back to listen as Stella read selected passages. Every now and then, Stella would look up, to see if she could tell from his facial expression what he was thinking about her writings, her views of the world.

She read him several vignettes about the town: a short piece on the Volunteers sitting in front of the firehouse; another on old Mrs. Shelton sitting on a bench in the square and spreading nasty gossip to whomever passed by; a comic sketch of Father Doheny giving his annual Church Building Fund speech; and finally a short story in the Gothic mode about a young girl who finds the ruins of the house of Usher.

Stella almost read her recent entry about looking at herself in the mirror, but chickened out. Closing the journal, she looked at him expectantly. Silent for a moment, Jamie looked up with eyes the color of autumn. Their gaze pierced her with dark intensity.

"What's the matter?" she asked. "Don't you like it?"

Jamie smiled and flushed faintly. "Oh, no. It's nothing like that. I was just trying to figure out how to say what I'm thinking."

"What do you mean?" Stella's heart thumped loudly in her chest.

"It's so good, Stella. *Really* good. I didn't know you . . . you did this. The writing, I mean. It's so full of *you!* Do you know what I mean?"

Stella smiled, and she felt herself blushing. "Yes," she said after a pause. "I think I do." She laughed nervously.

"No, it's true, Stella. I don't know what else to say. Those people, I mean, you've really got them down, just the way they are. Even if you hadn't mentioned their names, I would have still recognized all of them. It's like you were writing for *The Atlantic* or *The New Yorker*."

"You really think it's good?"

"Of course I do. That piece about the girl and the castle was really *magical!*"

Stella smiled, feeling a warmness rush through her. It felt so good to finally share what she felt.

"Jamie, have you ever liked any girls before?"

"What?" His expression changed, and he looked off-balance.

"You know, the way you like me. You *do* like me, don't you?"

Jamie laughed nervously. He looked so different, caught off-guard.

"Well, no," he said. ". . . I mean *yes*, of course I like you, Stella. And no, I never really liked any other girl—not like I like you, that is. I never really thought about getting to know any girls, until I started talking with you."

Stella smiled. "So you really want to get to know me better?"

"Yeah, I really do."

She looked at him and wondered if she was embarrassing him, if she was pushing too hard. She'd heard that you can't make an omelet without breaking some eggs, and with that thought firmly in mind, she pressed on.

"Jamie, do you think about me a lot? When we're not together, I mean."

"Yeah, I guess I do," he said, finding a sudden interest in the texture of the tablecloth.

"Am I embarrassing you?"

"No, not really. I've wondered the same about you."

She looked at him in silence for what seemed like a long time. "Have you ever thought about kissing me?"

He was unable to hide the surprise capering behind his eyes. "Yes, I've thought about it. But I never thought you would let me."

Stella got up on her knees and moved closer to him. She had embarrassed him, and his reaction only served to endear him more to her. "Oh, Jamie, I would let you. I *will* let you."

He moved close to her and she was powerfully aware of the tiny details of his face—the first traces of his beard, the thickness of his eyebrows, flecks of gold in his brown eyes.

She kept her own eyes open as he pressed his lips lightly against hers. Jamie closed his, and his long lashes danced hesitantly, as if he were unsure about keeping them shut. He started to pull away and she put one hand on the back of his neck, feeling his hair under her fingers, imprisoning him. Jamie responded and they kissed again, longer, and Stella felt a tingling sensation rush through her like electric current. It was so intense she didn't know if she could stand it.

Jamie opened his eyes and their gazes locked. He pulled back, still staring at her.

"Did you like it?" she asked gently.

Jamie could only nod his head.

"I didn't embarrass you, did I? I mean, I know the girl is supposed to wait for the boy to ask, and—"

"Oh, no," he said, trying to smile. "It's not that. I wasn't expecting it, and it was so *nice*, Stella. I've never kissed anyone like that before . . ."

"Neither have I," she said, feeling something new and bright take station in her breast. She loved the way he was so innocent, so honest.

She continued staring at him, and an awkward silence developed between them. Jamie sensed it and stood up, brushing off his blue jeans, looking at his watch.

"Gee, Stella, it's getting late. Maybe we ought to be getting back. Won't your aunt worry?"

She could tell that he was nervous, just making conversation, changing the subject. She said, "She won't worry until suppertime, Jamie . . ."

He looked away from her, not sure of their newly

attained intimacy. Turning, he spoke quickly. "I almost forgot, Stella. Some of the folks were talking about a new carnival wagon at church this morning . . . maybe we ought to go out and take a look at it?"

Stella knew that Jamie was only casting about for something to remove the pressure, but his mention of the carnival wagon had sent a sense of alarm through her mind. Until now, she had forgotten about the talk of the carnival man, the man in black with the strange shooting gallery. She wondered why Jamie had brought up such a subject. And yet, she was interested in the oddness of the gallery. She *had* intended to ask Jamie about it, and had merely forgotten.

"Do you really want to see it, Jamie?" She decided that she would like to see the gallery, as long as Jamie was sincerely interested. There was something about the carnival man which touched her imagination, her sense of the unknown.

"Yeah, I do," said Jamie. "I was going to mention it earlier, but we got kind of sidetracked, you know what I mean."

Stella paused, thinking more about what she really wanted to do. There was a magic peacefulness about the insect-humming stillness of the mill, and she enjoyed being alone with Jamie. She thought that she might like to kiss him again, to feel his arms holding her, his hands touching her. But she knew he was uncomfortable doing that, and she did not want to push him, to drive him away with her impulses. And suddenly she was thinking of the Williams boy, and how terrible it was, which reminded her of how much sadness and tragedy there was in the world. How selfish she was acting . . .

There would be plenty of time for her and Jamie. She promised herself that she would not force things. Maybe the carnival wagon would be a good idea.

"Yes, Jamie," she said after the thoughtful pause. "I think you're right. Let's go see what all the fuss is about. Help me with this stuff, okay?"

They packed the basket quickly and left the old mill. When they reached the stretch of black homes, Stella could feel the quiet mourning which hung over the area like a dark cloud. The ambulance was gone, and there was no sign of any of the tenants. Stella felt a grayness settle into her mind, replacing the joy she had experienced only an hour previously.

As they approached the center of town, it appeared almost deserted. No one sat on the square's benches, the shops and stores were all closed, their windows guarded against the coming night, blinds and shades like closed eyelids. Their footsteps echoed through the quiet streets, and Stella thought that even for a Sunday, Brampton seemed abnormally quiet. It was as if the town were hiding, or waiting for something to happen. It was an eerie sensation, and Stella wondered if Jamie also sensed it. She thought to ask him, but could not bring herself to speak.

They passed Wiggins' Texaco and continued down the main road toward the meadow. Stella attempted to order her thoughts. There were times, she knew, when she could not allow herself to ride out the impulses of pure feelings, times when she should stop to examine what was happening around her before acting. Jamie seemed to be like that almost all the time, and she admired him for it, because it gave him strength. She hoped that he admired her for her willingness to share with him. It was like Laura Gleesinger's book had suggested: Two people are sometimes able to share, and thereby learn from each other in special ways. Perhaps she could share her fears, as well as her joys, with Jamie . . .

Jamie touched her arm. "Look, Stella! There it is!" He pointed to a solitary black shape, squatting on the left side of the road. They approached the wagon slowly, suddenly aware of the lengthening shadows of afternoon. Stella looked at the wagon as they drew closer, impressed with its finely detailed beauty. Black as the night, the wagon proclaimed its rich American heritage with its white pinstripes and curlicues, its brass fittings and running lamps, and the bold white lettering trimmed in gold:

THE MAGNIFICENT GALLERY OF
MISTER MAGISTER

Jamie walked up to the back panel, which was folded up and locked by brass bolts. There was no sign of Mister Magister or the black horse. It was silent and still, which bothered Stella in a way she couldn't at first define. Then she knew what it was: There were no natural sounds—no wind, no insects, no birds.

"Wonder where he is," said Jamie.

"Magister?"

"Yeah. I heard everybody talking about how weird he looks. Probably part of his act."

"They said he wears black," said Stella. "Like an undertaker, or a magician."

Jamie did not answer, but continued to examine the wagon. He ran his fingers delicately over the lettering, touched the brass fittings, the wheels.

"You know," he said, turning to face Stella, "it's

funny . . . I've seen lots of carnivals come through here. Circuses and stuff like that. But I've never seen anything that looks like this."

"Yes, it's a beautiful wagon, isn't it?"

"No, I don't mean that," said Jamie.

"What do you mean?" Stella felt a chill pass through, afraid of what Jamie might say. Damn, she had a terrible imagination! she thought.

"Well, take a close look at this wagon," said Jamie. "It's so *clean,* like it was built yesterday. This paint's so bright and deep. Not a speck of dirt or road dust. The brass is all polished, and look at the wheels. They don't even look like they've been touching the road."

Stella studied the wagon. It *was* strange now that Jamie had mentioned it, had pointed it out. She was so taken with quaintness of the wagon that she would have never noticed such obvious oddities. She looked from the wagon to the surrounding country-side. It was so still, so desolate in the meadow. The air hung closely about them, silent save for their two voices. Stella wondered if nature was purposefully avoiding this place, and why . . .

"Hey, Stella, what's the matter?"

The sun's light had lost its warmth, and she felt a chill pass through her.

"I don't know, Jamie. It's kind of funny out here, don't you think? I keep thinking that maybe we shouldn't be here, alone like this. Mister Magister's not here. He might not like us poking around."

"Well, I don't know. I was thinking that maybe we should hang around till he comes back. You think he'll be open tonight?"

"I don't know. But I think we should leave. Please, Jamie?"

He looked at her and noticed the troubled look in her eyes, and though he did not seem to feel the oddness of the place as she did, he said, "Yeah, okay. Maybe you're right." He took her hand. "Come on, let's go."

Stella nodded, feeling the warmth of his grip, feeling instantly safer, more at ease.

They left the meadow, but after they'd gone only several yards down the road, Stella turned and looked back at the gallery. Its hard, dark edges looked out of place; it looked like a blackened hole cut into a pastoral canvas. Stella felt that it was an intruder, that it did not belong there in the bright meadow. She wanted to be away from the place as quickly as possible. Turning, she fell into Jamie's quick, rambling step, trying to shake the sharp impression that someone had been watching them.

CHAPTER 7

Word travels fast in this place, thought Magister.

He smiled as he gathered himself up from the darkness and walked to the front of his wagon. The young ones had retreated to the village, but they were replaced by an ever-growing crowd who came to the meadow to find some simple entertainment.

They were a gay and colorful lot, men and women of all ages and dimensions. They milled about the gallery, like drones returning to the hive, awaiting their turn at the counter. Magister watched their fingers dig deep into pockets, fumble blindly in purses. They drew out their tribute money and dropped the thin slugs into his Mason jar.

Their actions did not surprise him. He had seen this behavior countless times before. Different faces, different locations to be sure, but there were patterns which were universal, unavoidable.

Unless something special happened, someone extraordinary appeared.

The ugly duckling. The changeling. The mutant.

The crowd crackled with wonder and excitement.

The Magnificent Gallery had proved a sensation. An attraction beyond all reason.

Magister smiled as the shadows embraced him. Soon they would fall away from the counter like gluttons at a banquet, sated only because they were physically unable to continue.

But they would be returning.

CHAPTER 8

After he walked Stella to the front gate of her house, Jamie kept going down the block, and turned on Sycamore toward his own house. The big trees seemed to curl over the street, forming a tunnel of dappled earth-tone colors. Jamie walked along as if he were making his way through thick fog.

What was happening to him?

He couldn't get the image of Stella out of his mind. He couldn't stop re-creating the feeling of kissing her, of feeling electricity shoot through his body. Wow . . . no wonder people on TV and the movies made such a big deal over all that kind of stuff. It was *incredible*.

He kept wishing that the moment he had been kissing her could have lasted longer, that time could have somehow been slowed down, even that he could have stayed frozen in that single moment forever. It was the first time in his life that Jamie actually noticed how quickly time passed; never before had he felt the pang of losing something so utterly irretrievable.

He had the gut feeling that a milestone had just

been passed, and he knew in his heart that he would never forget this day, the day he kissed Stella Chambers. But why was he making such a big deal about it? To hear some of the guys talk in the bathrooms at school, you'd think that at fifteen, they were all getting laid like sailors on leave.

Maybe they were, and maybe they weren't, but Jamie knew that he himself had never even been kissed before, and that it was a big deal. Sometimes he had to chide himself for being so rational and analytical all the time.

He was glad that Stella had taken the initiative, because he was afraid he might never have done it himself. God, if she could have guessed how much he'd wanted to kiss her, to hold her and touch her. He wasn't sure it was so much an emotional attraction as much as just simple physical need. It seemed like all of a sudden, girls and pictures of women were very interesting to him, and he was getting hard-ons all day long.

Sometimes he lay in bed at night pondering the mysteries of sex, and he thought of Stella because she was the only girl he really talked to. Was that liking her or just lusting after her?

He didn't know, and at this point, it did not seem to matter, because if it always made you feel this good just *thinking* about sex, the whole scene must be great.

Looking up, he approached the hedge which bounded the property of his home. No one was sitting on the front porch, which meant that his father was probably watching the NFL game, and his mother was in the kitchen getting supper started. Funny, he could usually eat the hinges off the refrigerator, he was always so hungry around this time of day, but this evening, he wondered if he could eat anything at all.

After yelling out a brief greeting of "I'm home, Ma!" Jamie entered the house through the cellar door, which led him past the utility room, the laundry room, and a smaller space which he had staked out for himself. Jamie called the room his "workshop," but it was really more than that.

He had built some primitive shelving along one wall and filled it with his comics collection, and row after row of paperbacks on subjects which ranged from dinosaurs to interstellar nebulae. After reading somewhere that the slightly damp air normally found in basements was good for preserving the pages and bindings of books, Jamie had moved his whole library down from his bedroom to his workshop. He'd furnished the space with a stool and an old Formica kitchen table which served as a workbench, and here he built models from kits, designed little devices and things he called "inventions," and had played with his chemistry set and his microscope kit. The table was covered with the remnants of past projects; tools and materials lay scattered about in comfortable clutter. There was an old overstuffed chair in the corner of the room; a goosenecked reading lamp hung on the cinder-block wall from a masonry spike. That chair had been the seat in the cockpit of many an adventure for Jamie. He couldn't tell you how many nights he'd fallen asleep in that chair, a book draped across his chest.

Jamie liked this room. Despite its cool, somewhat dank atmosphere, it was a warm inner sanctum, a place where he could shut out the world and its craziness. He read in an article that by insulating the basement walls with some fiberglass batting and cheap paneling, he could reduce the heat loss by a factor 35 percent. If he did that, then maybe he wouldn't need the kerosene heater. As the days grew shorter and cooler, he often wished that he and his father would put up some inexpensive walls for his hideaway. But then, he would think, in a few years he would be moving out and going off to college, so then it wouldn't matter anyway.

He could put up with the cool temperatures for a few more winters. But the thought of going away to college made him think about how impermanent everything in life really was. It was hard to imagine a time when he wouldn't be down here in his special room, but that time was coming.

When he was younger, he and his father had built elaborate train "gardens" for his Lionel trains down in the basement, and each year it was an eagerly anticipated ritual—to get out the trains and create a miniature Brampton on the four-by-eight sheets of green plywood. During those years, Jamie couldn't dream of never setting up the trains again. But now that he was going on sixteen, they just didn't do it anymore. The trains sat in their dusty boxes, and Jamie and his dad had found other things to do together.

Things had changed.

And they would keep changing.

And now there was this thing with Stella getting started and he wondered if it was the signal for yet more changes in his life. Jamie sank down in the old stuffed chair, careful not to sit on the latest issue of *X-Men*. Someday he would sell his comics collection for huge sums of money, and use it to buy a big, solar-heated house. But he couldn't think about comics right now. In fact, he couldn't think about much of anything except how wonderful it had been to kiss Stella, and how his whole body had seemed to tingle with electricity.

Maybe he would ask his father about that feeling, if he could work up the nerve, and the timing seemed right.

He heard the kitchen door which led to the cellar steps open, and he knew what was coming next: "Jamie, it's time for supper!"

"Okay, Mom . . ."

"So put down whatever it is you're doing *right now*. It's on the table!"

"Okay, I'm coming."

He smiled as he mounted the stairs. His mom was so familiar with his ways. She always seemed to call him just when he was in the middle of something crucial, and he never seemed to be able to come up immediately.

"That was quick," said his mother as she looked over her shoulder to see him emerge from the darkness of the cellarway.

Jamie smiled and washed his hands in the sink. She had long ago given up the campaign to have him wash his hands in the bathroom, and now kept a dispenser of liquid handsoap on the countertop.

His mother was nearly forty, and she still looked great. Shoulder-length dark hair and dark eyes like his own gave her an intense, youthful look. And she kept herself in shape, working out with a couple of exercise tapes she played on the VCR, and riding the ten-speed bike he and Dad had gotten her two Christmases back. She wore jeans a lot, and didn't really look that much different from the girls in school. She worked as the photographer and graphics manager for the town's weekly newspaper, the *Brampton Bugle*. She loved taking pictures of things and her matted prints were hanging all over their house; sometimes she even sold one or two photos to some big magazines. Jamie was proud of her work and the way she looked. Some of the other kids' parents looked so *old*, so old-fashioned, so finished with the excitement of life.

Wiping his hands, he turned and headed into the dining room, where his father already sat at the head of the table. He was not a tall man, but he was sturdily built. A barrel chest and large powerful arms, which Jamie had not inherited, were hard to ignore, but he was not a brutish-looking man. His face, especially his eyes, conveyed a gentleness, a generous kind of understanding. He had thick dark hair and a ready smile, and a carefully trimmed mustache which gave him a kind of dashing aspect which Jamie had always liked. He had never seen his father without that mustache.

"Hello, son," said his father, reaching out and giving Jamie a friendly but firm tap on the biceps as he sat down. "Where've you been all day? Didn't you want to watch the game?"

"Yeah, I did. But I was out with Stella Chambers. We went on a picnic."

"Oh, yeah? A bunch of you kids?"

"Uh, no, it was just the two of us, really."

His father smiled and winked. "Down by the mill all by yourselves, eh?"

Jamie smiled. "Well, now that you mention it—"

"Get your elbows off the table, you two, and clear

me a place for this meat," said his mother as she entered the room carrying a platter with a half-carved roast lying in its own juices.

Jamie rearranged some of the vegetable dishes as she placed the platter on the table, then took her seat opposite Jamie. His father said a quick grace and reached for the meat.

"Stella Chambers," said his mother. "Isn't she the girl whose parents were killed in that car accident a few years ago?"

"Yeah," said Jamie. "Back when we were in the seventh grade. She lives with her aunt, right around the corner on Madison."

"That's right, I know her aunt—Leah Winter—she teaches at the elementary school."

"Uh-huh," said Jamie, realizing that he was hungry after all. He started serving himself from the various bowls and platters.

"She's a very pretty girl," said his mother.

"Yeah, I guess she is."

"You've been seeing quite a bit of her."

"Well, I guess so. Since this summer started. That's not all that long."

He was starting to feel embarrassed and hoped that the entire dinner conversation would not center on him and Stella. He looked at his father, who seemed to sense Jamie's discomfort with the situation as he grinned and nodded his head ever so slightly before speaking.

"Say, son, did you hear about that shooting gallery that came into town?"

Jamie was grateful for the change of subject, especially to one which interested him. "Yeah, I heard about it. I walked down this afternoon to take a look, but it was all closed up."

"Probably waiting for evening," said his mother.

Jamie nodded. He didn't want to get into how Stella thought the place was kind of creepy, or how the carnival wagon looked so new, and somehow so unreal in its newness.

"Mac called me this afternoon," said his father. "You know Mac McClelland from the plant, don't you?"

Jamie nodded as his father continued. "The plant" was the GTE electronics assembly building in the neighboring town of Garrison. Mr. McClelland was one of his father's coworkers at GTE. Jamie had met him on many occasions, usually when he would stop by to watch a game on TV or play some poker.

"Mac said he went down to that gallery last night and had a ball. What do you say we take a ride down there tonight?"

"It doesn't sound like much, honey," said his mother. "Just one wagon. Carnival was here at the end of August. What's just one attraction doing in town now?"

His father shrugged. "Who cares, really? It's going to be a beautiful night. Let's go, and maybe you can get some pictures for the *Bugle* while you're at it."

"That's true. All right."

"What about you, son? Want to come?"

Jamie did want to go along, but he had a feeling that whenever he went out there, he should do it with Stella.

"Nah, I don't think so. I'm working on a project, and I'd like to try to finish it tonight."

His father grinned. "You sure you just don't want to be seen with your parents?"

"No, Dad, it's not like that."

"I can remember when I was about your age. I didn't want to be caught *dead* with my father and mother . . ."

"No, no, it's not that—I like you guys, really," he said. "Maybe I'll go tomorrow night, okay?"

"Fine," said his father. "But Mac's going to stop by later, so we might as well go tonight, anyway."

Jamie nodded, and concentrated on his food. He and Stella hadn't talked about not going to the gallery separately, but somehow he had this feeling that this was the way she wanted it.

And he wanted what she wanted . . .

CHAPTER 9

Nils Johannsen was awakened by a soft, almost meek, knock at his door. It was a sound to which he had grown accustomed on Sunday mornings, and as he opened his eyes he anticipated the words which were to follow:

"Mr. Jo-*hann*-sen . . . ?" asked Alice Kirstin in a lilting, singsongy voice. "Breakfast is being served . . ."

"I be right down, madam," said Nils as he bounded out of bed buck-naked and pulled on a terry-cloth robe. Opening the door to the third-floor hallway, he could smell the rich aromas of brewed coffee, fried bacon, and fresh biscuits. Those smells always reminded him of home, back in Sweden. He saw that his landlady had already disappeared to the lower regions of the boardinghouse. She moved about the house as quickly and as silently as a cat, and Nils found that amazing, especially since he figured her age to be hovering somewhere in the sixties.

He padded down to the boarders' bathroom (house rules forbade him from using the facilities on the first or second floors) and closed the door. After relieving himself, brushing his teeth, and washing the sleep from his eyes, he returned to his room. He pulled on a flannel shirt, a pair of bib overalls, and moccasins for his feet. Now he was ready for a meal.

Sunday was Nils Johannsen's favorite day of the week. He savored the knowledge that it was Sunday as he descended the oak staircase. Sunday meant no work at Wiggins' garage, which also meant he did not have to get up at five-thirty in order to be on the job by six. Monday through Saturday, he caught a fast-food breakfast at the Hardee's on Union Street because Mrs. Kirstin didn't get up and start cooking until after eight.

Breakfast was included in the rent at the Kirstin Boardinghouse, but only if you could comply with the cook's schedule. It seemed fair to Nils. There was no reason why he should expect Mrs. Kirstin to get up two hours early just for him. He didn't even mind paying for the breakfasts he never got to eat. Life was not always fair, and he had learned to live with it.

Reaching the first floor, he entered the dining room where the other two boarders were already seated, drinking glasses of hand-squeezed orange juice and buttering toast.

"Good morning, gentlemen," said Nils with a smile. He brushed his blond bangs away from his eyes and took his customary chair by the window.

Old man Vardeman, isolated at the far end of the table, looked at him with a scowl and cleared his throat. Then he hocked up a mouthful of phlegm, which he spit into a coffee can he kept by the leg of his chair. Mr. Vardeman was a retired brakeman from the railroad, and his pension paid for his room and board and the few magazines and newspapers that he received in the mail. He was a thin, bent figure, with a gaunt skullish face and only a wispy suggestion of hair on his liver-spotted head. He had no family, no friends, and a sour disposition. He talked very little, but on those rare occasions, his sentences were always formed in the manner of complaints. He coughed almost constantly, and Nils had overheard Mrs. Kirstin tell a friend on the telephone that Mr. Vardeman was dying of emphysema.

"Good morning to ya, Mr. Johannsen!" said the other man, seated directly across from Nils.

His name was Jim Parker and he spoke with the drawl of a true Virginian. He had been living at the boardinghouse for almost as long as Nils' eight years, and he earned enough money to get by as the town handyman. If you needed your sidewalk recemented, or your porch roof mended, or maybe some built-in bookshelves for your den, or even a kitchen remodeled, Jim Parker was the man everybody in Brampton called. Jim was an easygoing talker with a thousand and one tales if you were patient enough to listen to them. He had traveled as a rigger with a one-ring circus when he was in his twenties and thirties and had never gotten over those days as "a rambler 'n' a gambler," as he would often say. His wife had run off with a traveling salesman about ten years ago, and after an ugly divorce, Jim had ended up at the boarding house.

"How you be feeling today this morning?" asked Nils as he reached for the frosted pitcher of juice and poured himself a glass.

Parker shrugged. "Good as I'll ever get, I reckon. Gonna lay back and watch some football this afternoon, then catch me a catnap, and then maybe go on down to that shootin' gallery everybody's talkin' about."

Nils smiled, nodded. "Ya . . . ya. Sounds goot." Parker had been trying to get him interested in American football for years, but despite his large, athletic-looking body, Nils had never been very interested in sports. All the men running in different directions never made much sense to him, but sometimes he would sit and watch a few minutes of a game with Parker just to have some company, just to be with someone who seemed to enjoy *his* company.

Jim Parker was one of the only people in town who really talked to Nils—really seemed interested in what he had to say. Nils knew that lots of people in town liked to imitate his accent, or the gangly, lumbering style of his gait, and that there were plenty of Nils Johannsen jokes about, and he knew that Jim Parker was not part of all that.

Nils was not actually a friend of Parker's, but at least the handyman was nice to him.

Just then Mrs. Kirstin emerged from the swinging door to the kitchen with a large platter of scrambled eggs, crisp bacon, and slices of scrapple.

"Good morning, Mr. Johannsen. Just in time."

She placed the big plate in the center of the table and all three men started helping themselves. This was usually the point at which Mrs. Kirstin would make her little self-amusing comment about the "boardinghouse reach," but this morning she kept it to herself. She was a large, fleshy woman with wide hips and an enormous bosom. Her features were pinched into the folds of her face. She reminded Nils of portraits and photographs of Slavic peasants, even to the way she wore her hair in a tight bun. Her manner was brisk and businesslike at all times, and although he had known her for more than eight years, he still had no idea what she really thought of him.

For the next few minutes everyone ate in silence. Mrs. Kirstin's personality might be a slab of cold indifference, but her cooking was superb. Nils filled his plate twice and was working on a second cup of coffee as Jim Parker studied the sports pages of the Sunday paper from Des Moines and old man Vardeman stared off angrily at the floral wallpaper patterns across the room. It was a typically quiet Sunday morning like so many others in Nils' life.

Whenever he thought about his situation, he found it crazy that he could be so alone when surrounded by people. How could he be lonely when he lived in a house full of others. And yet, all of them were strangers to him. They spoke at one another, but he did not know what any of them were feeling or thinking. His relationship with the others was like a game, a carefully worked-out ritual which everyone played with no passion or understanding.

Sometimes Nils wondered if it had been worth it to come to America in the first place. He had done so with a group of other mechanics to work in the planned American Volvo plant in Dubuque. When the deal fell through, many of his countrymen went back to Sweden, but Nils sensed a promise in this country that he could be happy and successful, and perhaps even wealthy.

The American Dream.

But so far, he had not found any streets paved

with gold, nor had he been able to achieve much measure of success. In his monthly letters to his sister, Leisa, who lived in Storskogsvagen, Nils told her of his problems in making real friends, in meeting women, in putting his life together. She responded by sending him books published in Swedish, Swedish newspapers, and letters which pleaded that he come home.

But he could not go home. He had made the decision to stay in this country and he was determined to succeed. Often he thought staying in a small town like Brampton had not been his best choice—but where could he go?

Over the years he'd attended lots of movies to learn English, and many of the films he'd seen about people coming to America took place in New York City. He thought about going to Manhattan many times, and even discussed it with his sister (who, of course, did not like the idea). But perhaps Brampton was too small for a man of his ambitions, and maybe New York City would be the best place for him.

Mrs. Kirstin invaded his daydreams by leaning over his shoulder to whisk away his plate and utensils.

"You finished, Mr. Johannsen?" she asked belatedly.

"Yes, I am," he said as she pushed through the swinging doors, ignoring him.

"Well, I'm going to take a walk," said Jim Parker, pushing back from the table. "Then the pregame show'll be comin' on . . ."

Mr. Vardeman hacked and hawked, made a deposit in his coffee can, and continued to stare at the opposite wall.

Nils decided it was time to go upstairs and get out his paints. Pushing away from the table, he moved to the kitchen door to thank Mrs. Kirstin and compliment her cooking. She replied with a short grunt, and continued cleaning up like a programmed piece of machinery.

Nils ascended the staircase to his room and retrieved his painting gear from the back of his closet. The walls of the rooms were covered with examples of his unframed works, and the back of the closet jammed with stretched, but as yet uncolored, canvases. Nils had loved painting with oils since he was no more than ten years old, but had only discovered the joys and ease of acrylics since coming to America. His style was inspired by the impressionism of people like Monet and Modigliani, and by the soft-edged realism of Wyeth. Nils liked to think that he had achieved a subtle blending of the·masters' styles to create a wholly original look.

As he set up his easel and began spreading and mixing some colors on his palette, he glanced around the room. So many paintings. Had he really done them all? Where had the vision and the energy come from? The thought of re-creating any of them seemed inconceivable, and yet one after another he continued to bring forth new canvases.

Every available space of wall had been covered by his paintings. Additional works lay stacked cheek to jowl on the floor and leaned in the corners of the room. Each one a rectangular slice of his existence, a measure of time and patience and vision.

Scanning some of his favorites, Nils realized that no one had ever seen his work, no one had ever shared his secret vision, his way of seeing the world.

It was possible that Mrs. Kirstin had seen them on her weekly forays into the room to change the bed linens, dust, and vacuum, but if she had ever noticed or appreciated his work, in eight years she had said nothing.

Nothing.

The idea of it pained him, and he shook his head slowly to banish the thought. How could a woman be so blind to the flash and fire of creativity? Did his work mean so little to her? Considering that her only concerns seemed to be clean towels in all the bathrooms and no dishes left in the kitchen sink, perhaps it was possible that his landlady was insensitive to the subtleties of art.

Nils smiled and began applying paint to the sky of his latest landscape—the east end of Brampton under the pall of a coming summer storm. It was a painting which emphasized the immensity of the sky, the power of nature, and the relative insignificance of man and his works. There was a raw sense of power and energy in the unfinished canvas, which seemed to command Nils to complete it.

And yet, as he worked, his mind kept returning to the fact that no one had ever seen his paintings.

It was a sin.

A crime. An unpardonable act, to which he himself was accomplice.

Despite his modesty and shyness there was a part of Nils which wanted recognition, which craved the praise of those who might appreciate his work—and his worth. And yet, what had he done to further this goal?

Hiding his work in a dark, gabled room. In shadowed corners and a black closet. God, how he wanted to hold up his work and simply ask people to look!

Maybe it was time, he thought.

Maybe he should stop dreaming of going to New York and starting over. Either he should pack his belongings and get on the next bus, or he should forget about it forever. Unless he started doing things differently, no one would ever see his work, and he would never learn the effects of his talent upon others.

Tomorrow, thought Nils with a new resolve.

Tomorrow my life changes.

"Another day closer to the end, Sophie," said Eli Liebowitz, looking up at a sepia-toned photograph of a young woman from a younger time. Eli sighed and continued to pace about the crowded little room, which had the shabby grace of an eastern European sitting room.

Large pieces of furniture, designed for rooms far larger than his, loomed all around. Photographs of his son and two daughters, and of course his darling Sophie, all in gilded frames, littered the tops of every table and even filled in the spaces in an oaken bookshelf. Eli was not even certain he liked having all those pictures around all the time. They only served to remind him of times long past. Times long dead.

But Sophie had loved the photographs and had made a great fuss over where to place each new one. And so, for Sophie, Eli kept the pictures arranged just as she had wanted them.

Sophie. Almost three years, and he still could not believe she was really gone. The years jumped past you with such frightening speed. Some days were like the blink of an eye, punctuated by his climbing into a solitary bed, wondering if he would again see morning.

But Sundays were not like the rest. Sundays were the slowest days of all, and in another sense, the most cruel. Eli assumed this was because he did not work on Sundays—something this Christian-dominated town would never tolerate—and also because Sunday had been the day when his family would gather at their house on Franklin Street.

Settling down in his favorite chair, Eli found himself smiling as he remembered those days. Ah, the laughter which filled the old house back then! The sounds of children, of meals being cooked in the big kitchen, of the arguments and discussions about Russian history which Sophie would inevitably initiate.

But the children grew up, married and moved away, had children of their own. His youngest daughter had married a Gentile boy (a *Catholic*, yet!), and they lived with four children in the hideous sprawl called Los Angeles. Eli had visited them once and swore never again! His son had become an engineer and worked for NASA in Houston, and his first daughter, the one who looked so much like Sophie, had married a boy who became an art gallery agent in Manhattan (another snake pit!). Scattered like leaves, his children were. The grandchildren he never saw, other than the pictures they sent. Despite the geographic differences, the pictures looked like they were taken by the same school photographer. When Sophie lived, the two of them had attempted to traverse the country at least once a year to see everyone, but in three years Eli had not left the city limits of Brampton. He rarely even called any of them.

The house on Franklin Street, which at one time had been so cozy, so crowded, had suddenly become a monstrously huge and empty place. He had sold it below market value just to get out as quickly as possible, and had taken the tiny apartment in the rear of his shoe repair shop. Unable to discard any of the gatherings of a lifetime, Eli had jammed it all into the little apartment, like storage in a warehouse. The place was like his mind—cluttered with the junk of seventy-two years. He had little use for any of it, but it was simply there.

During the week, he sat in the dark shadows of the shop, mending shoes and doing the odd leather-repair, speaking to no one unless a customer spoke first. When he thought about it, he decided he must look like a stooped and twisted little troll, hunched in a corner, scowling and glaring at any who might invade the darkness of his lair. The image struck him funny and he laughed into the silence of a Sunday afternoon.

"A troll, Sophie . . . That's funny, isn't it?"

Getting up, he moved to the galley kitchen in the rear of the apartment and put on water for some tea. He collapsed upon a kitchen chair and watched the flames lick the kettle's bottom. The fire started him thinking the old thoughts again. He turned his head away, but the old memories started taking shape in his mind, not to be ignored.

Black-and-white memories. Like tattered old newsreels, images of Nazi soldiers, cattle cars, and herded packs of undesirables flickered in the screening room of the past. Eli was a young man, a guildsman, with a very young wife and one-year-old son when the soldiers came into his home (on a Sunday, yet!) and took them to a processing center near the railroad yards outside of Pribor. When he saw all his neighbors and friends and even some of his relatives also collected at the center, he knew what was going to happen to them.

It had been a cold November night when the train came. The air was so cold it captured the breath of the soldiers as they stood silhouetted against the yard's signal lights. Roughly, the Jews were prodded and pushed into the stinking cars, cars with hay-strewn floors which smelled of shit and piss and vomit from previous passenger loads. They were forced into the cars in such numbers that the passengers could do nothing but stand, wedged against one another like upright cords of stovewood.

And in a sense, that's what many of them became.

Eli remembered his young wife, clutching the baby to her breast, reaching a pale white arm through the press of bodies to touch him. That touch, against the sleeve of his coat, had been enough to give him strength. He could not see her in the darkness, could not hear her above the roaring clatter of the train's wheels, but her touch sustained him.

They rode for eighteen hours standing up with no food and no sleep, and some of them died before even reaching the camp in Belsen. But Eli had been a strong, athletic young man, and it would take more than a train ride to kill him. It would, in fact, take more than the Nazis kept within their arsenals of hate and destruction.

But they did their best.

After being registered at the Belsen camp, the men were separated from the women, and Eli never saw his young wife again. Because he was so strong and full of shrewdly quiet intelligence, the soldiers soon offered him one of the *capo* jobs, and he accepted it only because the possibility of increased privileges meant he might be able to see his wife again, or at least get the knowledge that she was alive.

But that knowledge never came. He worked hard and he oversaw his peers with a silent strength that many of them did not admire or want. As he watched the inmates march off to dig their own mass graves, to take the death showers, he became more and more determined to live, to see the end of the nightmare. For even then, Eli was wise enough to know that nothing lasted forever, not even the Third Reich. And so he guarded his strength and his importance in the hierarchy of prisoners, and was never tapped for elimination when the doctors and the lieutenants made their rounds.

And as quickly as the years now passed, back then they moved with a glacial slowness. Three years were three eternities, but the day came when the sound of distant thunder burst over the horizon. Allied thunder. It was like an approaching storm which never subsided, and if he closed his eyes, Eli could vividly see the Nazi soldiers as they packed their gear and deserted the camp like roaches rousted from their nest. They left the rows of barracks, niveous bone-yards, and still-smoldering ovens to be found by soldiers from an America ignorant of such horrors.

Eli remembered the stunned, slack-jawed faces of

the GIs who first entered the camps and found the skeletons of both the living and the dead. He remembered how most of the prisoners just stood in their putrid stalls and hovels when the gates were thrown open, as though the concept of freedom had lost all meaning for them. But for Capo Liebowitz, it had been a joyous day, the day he had lived for.

He was befriended by an American soldier from a place called Iowa, a young man named Frankie Harris. The soldier filled his head with visions of a dreamland called America, where there were fields of wheat and corn, which rolled and pitched like a vast ocean as far as the eye could see, where everyone loved each other, and every man could choose his own destiny. Frankie Harris helped him get the necessary papers, and within six months he was on a freighter bound for Ellis Island.

Beneath the shadows of the bright, tall buildings, many New Yorkers labored in the cramped, dreary quarters of generations past. Eli marveled at neighborhoods which railed with foreign accents, stewed in the juices and cured in smells of other lands. It was a Little Europe, and he wondered how much of his life he had really left behind. But he worked hard and he lived with a mean frugality which sustained him. It felt so good to be alive.

For two years he apprenticed at a shoe shop in Brighton Beach in Brooklyn. On one of those days in one of those years a beautiful girl named Sophie Segal entered the shop to have her dancing shoes reheeled. They were married three months later, and soon afterward, he received a letter from his liberator and patron, Frankie Harris. The ex-soldier was back in Garrison, Iowa, where he worked with his father on the family farm, but he had never forgotten Eli. Frankie traced him down and now wrote to invite him for a visit and to tell him that the neighboring town of Brampton was in need of a shoe repair shop.

The dream was kindled, and Eli let its flames consume him. He and his wife deserted the comfortable ethnic neighborhoods of Brooklyn and entered the country's heartland. They found a place where few, if any, of the people had ever *heard* of a Jew, much less ever seen one. It was a place where the nearest synagogue was almost a two-hour drive but there were churches on every corner.

And yet it had been a good place to raise a family, even if the children seemed to become more a part of the town than their parents could hope to do. Eli had never cared about any subtle inconformities between his home and all the others on the block. He did not try to be different from them, he simply was.

And when he was a proud and angry young man, he reveled in those differences. He flaunted them and perhaps paid the price for his arrogance. As he grew older, and mellowed, and became more conservative in his views of the world, he wished that he could have not alienated so many people. Perhaps things would have been a little easier.

The kettle whistled and screamed, jarring him from his memories, and Eli moved to get a teabag from the canister on the counter. Turning off the flame, he shook his head and wondered whether it had all been worth it. What good did it do to work so hard, only to see your family break off from you and go away? What good did he serve now, just marking off the days?

The ringing phone shattered his fragile thoughts, and he left the tea steeping as he picked up the receiver. What could this be? No one ever called him, especially on a Sunday.

"Yes? Who is it?"

"Daddy? It's Sarah! How are you?"

The sound of his baby girl's voice warmed him like the breath of early summer, soothed him like a eucalyptus balm. He felt himself smiling and nodding, and suddenly, it had become a very nice day indeed.

CHAPTER 10

This is one hell of a crowd, thought Sam Havens as he pulled his beat-up Camaro onto the shoulder of the state highway leading out of town. Sundown just comin' on, and there were already long lines of cars parked on both sides of the road.

Thinking back to August, when the whole carnival was spread out across the meadow, Sam didn't remember more cars then than were there right now. He walked up the gravel shoulder, looking at all the familiar faces gathered around the wagon. Sam spotted Doc Ames, the veterinarian, and his wife, Sarah; and wasn't that Bill Holbrook, the salesman for John Deere? It sure looked like him. And coming up the other side of the road was Dom Costa, who managed the Food Mart, with his whole family in tow. Jesus, how could a man stand to have all those children goofin' around him all the time?

A couple of enterprising kids had set up a lemon-ade stand on the roadside, and people were just kind of flowing from the stand to the gallery and then ebbing out into the space between the two. Sam figured that sooner or later, he'd see just about everybody he knew.

Way off between a couple of trees stood Mister Magister. He was brushing down the biggest, blackest stallion Sam had ever seen, but the carnival man didn't seem to be paying much attention to the horse. Even though Magister's face was hidden under the droopy brim of his hat, Sam had a feeling the man was watching the goings-on at the gallery.

Hell, Sam couldn't blame him for that. If it was his investment, he'd sure be watching them quarters piling up in that jar.

A quarter. Now, that was funny, 'cause Sam had a feeling that even if Magister had charged everybody a dollar, they'd all still be out here waiting to take their turns.

Sam moved to the lemonade stand, bought a big cup, then ambled slowly toward the gallery itself. There was a pack of the regular guys from Donnegan's Taproom bunched up to the right of the wagon. They were all laughing and talking and waiting their turn as Sam joined them.

"Hey, grease monkey!" said Red Lauterbach, a tall, thin man with carrot-orange hair and a scraggly beard the same color. "I hear you're a pretty fair shot on this thing!"

Sam grinned. It made him feel good to think that word of his shooting got around so quick. It was nice to have people know neat stuff about you. It made him feel like a real somebody.

"I can shoot a fly offa bull's nuts at fifty yards," said Sam. "Or offa yours, if you want."

All the guys laughed. Some of them elbowed Red Lauterbach, daring him to take Sam up on his claim, but Red just guffawed and shook his head.

"You were up here last night, weren't you, Sam?" asked Cy Hartwell. Cy raised corn a couple of miles outside of town.

"Yep," Sam beamed. He felt like a real celebrity having beat them all to the punch. "Weren't half as crowded as it is tonight."

"Word's got around that it's a good show," said Red.

Sam stole a quick glance at the counter, where some teenagers were taking their shots, then back at his small audience. "Hell, yes, it's good! I'm tellin' ya, you guys've never seen nothin' like this one."

"Shit," said Cy. "It's just a shootin' gallery. What's the big deal?"

Sam grinned. "It ain't no sense in me tryin' to tell you what it's like. You'll see for yerself . . ."

"Well, what do you say," said Red Lauterbach, "let's get up there and get in line."

"Everybody'll get their turn," said Sam. "Don't worry about that."

And he was right. Though the evening wore on and more and more people pulled up in their cars to see what the commotion was all about, the crowd never got rough or pushy. Nobody ever got impatient, and nobody seemed to hog time at the counter. It seemed like everybody took just enough shots to—

Sam wasn't sure how to describe it. Enough shots to what? To satisfy themselves? To hit all the targets? To get the job done. Yeah, maybe that was it.

What the hell was he thinking about? What job? It wasn't no job when you were just havin' fun, was it?

Sam tried not to think about things like that because it always ended up getting him confused, and when he got all confused he started feeling agitated, and when he got agitated he usually got his ass in some kind of trouble. So he'd found through trial and error (mostly error, and one or two trials even) that he should try to keep from making himself feel confused in the first place.

But there was no impatience in the crowd. Everybody seemed real content, knowin' that the wagon was out there for them, and that they would all get their chance.

It was a comforting feeling. That was the only way you could put it. Looking up, Sam again saw Magister standing off in the shadows of the trees—away from the crowd, but close enough to keep an eye on things. Once again Sam had the creeping feeling that the man in the black hat and cape was staring right at him.

It was a funny feeling, like the way he felt one time as a kid in the old five-and-ten-cents store when he was stealing a glow in the dark Yo-Yo and he turned around and there was old Mrs. Standish looking right at him. Sam could remember that just like it was yesterday. The hand holding the Yo-Yo was right down by his pocket, and he was just ready to stuff it in when he looked up and saw the old woman. His face had started to feel real hot and he knew he must have looked guilty as hell. He put the Yo-Yo back in the rack and ran out of the store as fast as he could.

It was weird, but he had the same kind of feeling when he felt Magister staring directly at him. But unlike so many years ago in the dime store, Sam did not have the urge to run. Though he felt like he had just been caught doing something wrong, his reaction was different this time. He wasn't exactly sure what the wrongness was, what he had been caught doing . . . And thinking like that would start making him feel confused, so he figured he just better quit wondering and maybe think up a couple of good jokes to tell the guys.

And so Sam stood his ground behind the rest of the main clot of people, gradually easing closer and closer toward the counter. His buddies orbited around him as he kept them amused with some of the latest jokes he'd heard from people passing through the gas station. He was always good at telling jokes (at least everybody seemed to laugh real good), and when he got to the punch line of the one about the guy who came into the bar with a trained baboon, they all roared their approval.

As the laughter subsided, Cy Hartwell let his eyes roam casually over the crowd, and Sam noticed his half-grinning expression suddenly change to one of concern.

"What's the matter, Cy?" he asked.

Hartwell looked at him beneath his yellow Cat baseball cap, shrugged. "Don't know. I thought that carnival fella was watchin' me, you know? Like he had his eyes right on me, and when I looked over at him, damn if it don't look like he was doin' just that!"

Sam nodded and glanced at Magister, who did seem to be looking in their direction. But the light and shadows were tricky, and you couldn't really see his eyes, so you couldn't be sure . . .

"Ah, you can't tell for sure," he said, slapping Cy on the shoulder. "With that big hat hanging down, you can't even see his eyes."

"Yeah, I know," said Cy Hartwell. "That's what's kinda buggin' me, you know?" There was a moment in which none of them spoke, and it was an awkward, almost scary moment.

Some of the people at the counter put down their guns and slipped away through the crowd. Those closest to the wagon eased up to the fold-down board, plinked their quarters into the Mason jar, and picked up the rifles. Sam and his cronies inched closer.

"Hey," Sam said, dispelling the weird feelings. "We're next!"

"Yeah," said Red Lauterbach as he peered between the hunched shoulders of two of the shooters in front of him. "What's it look like in there?"

"It's amazin'," said Sam.

"Can't see shit from here," said Red, rubbing his beard. "Looks dark and empty."

"It ain't," said Sam. "When you get up to the counter, your view gets better. You can see everything."

"Wonder how he does it?" mused Cy Hartwell.

"It's probably some kinda optical delusion," said Sam.

Tilden Strong turned off the key in his car's ignition and sat for a minute reflecting on things. His wife and daughter were already out the doors, looking toward the crowd at the meadow. What a difference from last night, he thought with bemusement.

Sometime during the day, Joanna had been informed by way of her womanfriends' telephone grapevine that it was okay to come out to see the shooting gallery, and had therefore insisted on coming with him tonight. Tilden smiled ironically. Suddenly, because Joanna now wanted to be there, her suggestion from last night (that a carnival wagon was not fit entertainment for "a man of his age") was void.

Louisa ran off from the car to join a gaggle of her high school friends, as Joanna leaned into the car to glare at her husband.

"Well, are you coming or not?"

"Yes, I'm coming," he said. He opened the door and slipped out.

The air was cool, but it was not yet edged with winter. The moon was high and bright. It was a good night to be out under the stars. He joined Joanna and walked toward the crowd. Some kids had put up a lemonade stand, and it looked like Tom Donnegan had dragged out his hot-dog stand and portable generator. There were some colored light bulbs strung across the branches of two trees above the steaming aluminum frankfurter cart, and to Tilden, the scene had a truly carnival air.

Almost immediately, as they drew closer to the crowd, Joanna spotted one of her friends and moved off to greet her. Tilden gravitated along with her.

"Hello, Mary. Is John with you?"

"Yes, he's up there with Liz and Little John, waiting their turns." The woman looked at Tilden and smiled thinly. "Hello, Til. Sorry to hear about your delivery boy."

He didn't understand what she had said. "What?"

"Didn't you hear?" The woman seemed surprised.

"Hear what, Mary? I've been home all day."

"Oh, Tilden, that's right," said Joanna. "I forgot to tell you!"

"Would one of you mind telling me now? What's this about my delivery boy? Clarence? Or Timmy?"

"Clarence," said Joanna, her aging face abruptly

taking on a serious expression. "I forgot to tell you that he died this afternoon."

"Yes," said Mary. "His mother called the 911 number, but it was too late. He just up and died is what I hear."

"What happened to him?" Tilden heard himself asking the question, but his thoughts were racing ahead, making connections, observations. Although a part of him was shocked to discover a young boy had died, there was another part which accepted the news with a cool knowledge, as though it were somehow expected.

He was surprised, and yet he was not. Nor should anyone who had been paying attention these last couple days.

"That's just terrible," he said softly. It was an automatic response, which masked his deeper feelings about the news. He was scared.

Mary shrugged. "Well, you never know what was *really* going on, you know. A boy like him could have been fooling around with drugs or something. You just never know, Joanna."

"That's right," said his wife.

A boy like him. Mary's phrase echoed through Tilden's head.

Something strange was happening, and he wondered if anyone else had noticed.

CHAPTER 11

Stella had always felt that Sunday nights were a funny time of the week. They usually marked the end of a lazy day in which not much had happened or gotten accomplished. Sunday nights were a time for catching up on neglected weekend homework, and a reminder that Monday was coming, and with it a long week of school before the freedom of another weekend. But this Sunday had been different because of the beautiful time she spent with Jamie, and even, she thought a bit grimly, because Clarence Williams died.

But she tried not to think about it as she finished a book from her English class's summer reading list and laid the novel on her desk. She still had almost an hour before she ought to go to sleep, enough time to write a few pages in her journal and maybe read another chapter of *The Facts of Life and Love*.

She picked up the book and spent half an hour reading about precautions to take so that you wouldn't become pregnant. Just thinking about that happening made her feel a bit queasy. God, it would just *kill* Aunt Leah—and what would Stella do in such circumstances? The idea of having a baby when you were just a teenager seemed crazy, and yet having an abortion was more than unthinkable to her. She'd seen many news reports on the pro- and anti-abortion coalitions and demonstrations and had formed her own opinions about the practice. It seemed like killing a living being to her, and that was just plain wrong. That's all there was to it.

The rest of the chapter was concerned with making the decision about having sex with someone, and what questions to ask yourself, questions which might reveal why you were doing it in the first place. To Stella, the whole subject was mysterious and exciting, but also very scary. Just reading about sex made her curious, but it also made her wary. She wondered if all the kids in her class felt the same way, or if she was the only one who was mystified and confused.

Sometimes she felt confident and determined to do some experimenting with her new feelings; at other times, she felt baffled and almost terrified to even think of trying anything.

When she felt this confused, she found herself wishing that she was already a grown woman and that this part of her life was behind her. But that would mean that all the wonder and beauty of discovery that Laura Gleesinger wrote about would also be behind her. The author stressed her belief that adolescence did not have to be an awkward, distressing time if a person approached all problems with an open mind, healthy curiosity, and an appreciation of the many pitfalls awaiting all teenagers, and Stella found her attitude very encouraging.

Finishing the chapter, Stella picked up her journal and wrote a brief summary of the day's events, then commented on each incident. She tried to make the walk down Grover's Road read like a short story. She reported the tragedy at the Williams house as though it were an article in *Time*. And then she wrote about Jamie.

It was just sinking in that she had trusted him this afternoon with a part of her life no one had ever glimpsed before. Reading to him from her journal was like letting him into her mind to share her most secret thoughts. She wondered if that sharing was somehow more important than letting him into her body. The thought posed an interesting philosophical question. The more she pondered the whole thing, the more apprehensive she became, wondering if she had acted too rashly in letting Jamie into her inner world.

And yet, she felt this need to share her thoughts and feelings with someone. And she believed she could trust Jamie, really trust him. He seemed like a special person, not at all like the other boys. It was not just his intelligence which inspired her trust but also his sensitivity and his sense of wonder in the world.

She finished her journal entry with a description of her feelings at the meadow when she and Jamie had gone down to see the carnival man and his shooting gallery. She found it odd that this "Mister Magister" would come to town all alone, and almost a month after the regular carnival had been through.

And his wagon was drawn by a horse. It was almost as if he had rolled into town not only from another place but from another time.

The thought gave her pause. Stella looked at the sentence she had written over and over. A shudder passed through her as though a sudden draft had slicked through her bedroom, and she glanced up to ensure that her window was closed tightly. There was something about the appearance of the carnival man which she found discomforting. Something was amiss.

It was an especially odd feeling when she considered how excited the rest of the town seemed to be. Even Aunt Leah had heard some of the talk about the shooting gallery. It seemed to be immensely popular, and that in itself should have dispelled any feelings of alarm or dread which preyed upon her imagination.

But it did not.

Maybe Jamie would know something. She looked at the newly installed telephone which her aunt had given her. It was a present given for no obligatory reason like a birthday or Christmas, and Stella had found she valued it more because of that.

She dialed Jamie's number and hoped that it was not too late to be calling.

"Hello?" a woman's voice answered. Stella could not detect any suggestion of annoyance in her voice. Still, she spoke quietly.

"Hello, Mrs. Rodin, this is Stella Chambers. I'm not calling too late, am I?"

"Oh, hello, Stella! No, it's not too late. Did you want to talk to Jamie?"

"Yes, ma'am. He's still up, isn't he?"

Mrs. Rodin chuckled. "Jamie? He's down in the basement in that workshop of his. He'll be up for hours yet. I don't know when that boy ever sleeps, but he gets up on time every morning!" She laughed again.

Stella laughed, too, remembering how Jamie had once told her that people sleep an average of one third of their lives, and ever since then, he had tried to sleep less because he didn't want to waste so much time doing nothing.

"Hang on, Stella, and I'll get him . . ."

Stella waited in silence, anticipating the sound of Jamie's voice, then heard footsteps approaching the phone, followed by:

"Hi, Stella, what's up? I was just thinking about you."

"Really? That's nice, Jamie. I was just writing some stuff in my journal and I was thinking about you, too. I wanted to talk to you about this afternoon."

"Yeah. The picnic was great. We should do it again before it gets too cold."

"Yes, it was fun," she said, then paused to clear her throat. He sounded so effervescent all the time, so full of energy, that it made her smile in spite of the serious question she wanted to ask him. "But I was thinking about when we went out to the meadow to see Mister Magister's gallery. Remember?"

"Sure. Why?"

"I don't know. It's just that when I was thinking about it just now, I had a funny feeling. Sort of a creepy feeling—and I was wondering if it affected you the same way."

"Gee, Stella, I don't know. It's kinda weird, I guess."

"When we were out there," she said softly, as if there were others she did not want to hear her speaking, "I had this feeling that we were being watched."

"Really?"

"Yes. Even though we didn't see Magister around anywhere, maybe he was there anyway, and he was watching us."

"Yeah, that is creepy. I see what you mean."

"Did you feel anything like that? That's really why I called," she said. "I wanted to know if it was real, or if it was just me and my imagination."

Jamie was silent for a moment, then let out a long, slow breath. "I don't know, Stella. To be honest with you, I didn't notice anything that weird."

"Oh . . ."

"Hey, I mean, it's weird enough that that guy would be here this late in the year, you know?"

"Yes, I thought about that," she said.

"But lots of people have been going down there, and they've been having fun. My father went tonight with some of the guys from where he works. He wanted me to go with them."

"Did you go?" A pulse of excitement went through her.

"Nah, I wanted to fool with some stuff down in the cellar."

"Uh-huh."

"Plus, I figured that maybe you and I could go down one night this week. It might be neat."

Stella's heartbeat accelerated, and she smiled into the phone. "Oh, Jamie, that would be nice. I'd like that."

She wanted to say that she would feel safe with him, but he might think she was being silly. She subtly changed the conversation and they discussed the coming school year, figuring out that they could meet during the day at lunch in the cafeteria and after school in the town library. Classes would begin in just a few days, and they were both looking forward to the excitement of the year.

Hanging up the phone, Stella felt comfortable with the bond which was growing stronger and stronger between her and Jamie. She found herself smiling as she cleaned up her desk, put away her journal, and replaced *The Facts of Life and Love* in her sweater drawer.

She dressed for bed, then turned out the lights and slipped under the bedcovers. Broken moonlight entered at the window and speckled the wall by her bed. Stella found herself staring at the latticework of shadow and light, looking for images and shapes the way she had when the guidance counselor at school asked her to see things in his batch of ink-blot cards. But this was different—the wind soughed through the trees outside, making the branches move, making the shadows on the wall also move. The shapes were always changing and, thus animated, assumed a different, darker aspect.

The shadows metamorphosed from twisted limbs into arms and claws which seemed to be ever-reaching. Great eyes blinked from monstrous heads, then changed and flowed and shifted into wings and tails, into slouching bodies, hulking blobs.

The effect was mesmerizing, and Stella had to force herself to turn away, to bury her head in her pillow and try to forget what she had seen. Her previous good feelings had abruptly deserted her, and no matter how hard she tried to recapture them by thinking of Jamie, she could not. Her warm mood had been shattered with the invasion of the shadows, and she tried to escape by retreating into sleep . . .

But tonight there was no ease in sleep.

She stood on a hill, looking down into a shallow valley where a town lay close to the night. It was very dark and the vault of star-filled sky seemed infinitely far away, making her and all about her seem insignificant. A cruel, cold mist snaked through the town in the valley, touching each house on each street with a serpentine foulness. Stella watched the living fog move with a slow but inexorable stealth, and she was reminded of a disease, as it was passed from victim to victim.

As she watched the town become infected by the mist, she knew that she was looking at her own town of Brampton. Her vision became telescopic, and although she stood far away, removed and safe from whatever it was that contaminated the town, she could suddenly see into every street, up to the front porches and windows of every house. The vision had the vague-but-crisp reality of all dreams. Stella knew that what she saw was not possible, yet it was perfectly acceptable.

Stella watched.

The vapors which fingered through the streets had snaked up the walk of Jamie's house, had streamed through the window glass like barbecue smoke through a screen door. As the mist entered the house, the lights inside blinked out, and Stella felt a pang of ache in her breast.

She felt herself gliding forward, barely touching the earth with her bare feet. A warm, humid breeze, like the breath of an unseen animal, washed over her, fluttered the long satin nightgown she wore.

Stella descended into the valley, entered the streets of the town. The vapor seemed to disappear as she drew closer to her own street, the walk of her aunt's house. As she reached the front porch, she detected movement in the extreme periphery of her vision, and turned to look back.

And there it was, at the end of the street, rolling forward, crashing and retreating, then advancing again, like the breakers of a ghostly sea. The fog closed in. Stella could see shapes and textures within the roiling cloud. Dark bodies and glowing coals which might be eyes churned and boiled in the depths of the cool smoke. The sounds of wailing and despair and untold pain filled the night, but the sounds were muffled, as if the vapor were absorbing the sound, keeping it within. Stella's dreaming mind formed the image of a great ectoplasmic blob, an amoebic creature which had absorbed the souls of everyone in the town and now rolled on, carrying the damned within its heart, an ever-traveling hell.

The mist rolled toward her, reaching the front walk, coming up the path, reaching for her, hungrily.

Stella wanted to move, but found herself rooted to the spot. Trying to scream produced only a feeble squeak, a hoarse nothing of a sound.

The vapor paused for an instant, a phosphorescence pulsing within its depths.

Stella knew that whatever this thing was, she would not be allowed to run from its shapeless mass. As it grew closer, the muffled sounds of the damned grew more distinct, though no louder than before. The first fingers of mist humped and twisted up the front porch steps, encircling her ankles with an arctic touch. The shock of such utter coldness shattered her dream paralysis and she screamed—and awoke staring at the ceiling. There was a patina of sweat on her face, and her heart labored, thumping in her chest.

What was happening to her?

CHAPTER 12

Joseph Dutton leaned against the bar and surveyed the situation. He was more than a bit surprised.

For a Monday night, he'd have to say that Tom Donnegan's Taproom was downright crowded. Every booth was filled with men accompanied by their lady friends or their wives, and the bar was ass-deep in guys from one end to the other. He'd never seen it like this except on a Friday or Saturday night, or maybe on the Fourth of July.

And he knew there was only one reason for it: the Magnificent Gallery of Mister Magister. He could've told Donnegan there was going to be a mob in here tonight. Dutton knew that everybody and their brother would be packin' the place to talk about that contraption.

"Hey, Dutton, where's the old lady?" asked Chuck Grant, who smiled as he nudged him with his elbow. Grant managed the feed and grain store and was one of Dutton's card-playing, hard-drinking, cathousing buddies. He was a tall, gangly man of about forty-five, with small bird-shot eyes and a very unprominent chin that receded into his neck. Chuck was losing his hair at an alarming rate, and Dutton figured he was going to look funny bald.

Dutton snorted across the top of his beer mug, sending a spray of foam into the air. "I sent her along home. Millie ain't crazy about this place, and I told her I was thirsty."

Chuck Grant nodded. "You betcha, good-buddy," he said as he stared at a girl of perhaps nineteen or twenty sitting in the booth directly opposite their spot along the bar. "This ain't no place for wives when there's young stuff like that hangin' around."

The girl wore very tight jeans and a bright yellow leotard top. Her young breasts pushed against the stretch material. Dutton had been watching her ever since she'd come in with another girl and two long-haired studs barely out of high school.

Couple of lanky dirt-balls, he thought. What the hell did they know about women? How could a couple of ugly creeps like that end up with a woman like her?

"How'd you like to give her some of the old beef injection, Mr. Butcher-man?" Chuck Grant guffawed as he nudged Dutton again.

Dutton hitched up his belt over his forty-six-inch belly, looked at his friend, and smiled. "Maybe I will, one of these days . . ."

Grant laughed. "Yeah, sure, Joe! What would she want with a big hog like you?"

"My big hog . . . you said it."

And they both laughed at that one, then finished off their mugs in one final swallow.

Joseph signaled for refills as he scanned up and down the bar. Several stools down, he spotted Sam Havens yammering away with his two layabout friends, Red Lauterbach and Cy Hartwell. Talk about the three stooges; their combined IQ probably didn't equal the weight of any *one* of them.

Bunky, the barkeep, slid two new frosted mugs into their hands, whisked away the spent ones. After they had both taken another swallow, Chuck nudged him again. It was an irritating habit which Dutton had gotten used to over the years. Shit, nobody's perfect, right?

"Yeah, what?" asked Joseph.

"I been thinkin'," said Grant.

"That's kinda dangerous, ain't it?" He grinned and continued to watch Yellow Leotard's nipples try to poke through the fabric.

"Cut the shit."

"Okay, shoot," said Joseph.

"I seen you over at Harker's meadow tonight. What d'you think of that shootin' gallery?"

Joseph sighed. "To tell you the truth, even that young pussy over there can't keep it out of my mind."

"Really? You, too?"

"Yeah."

"Wonder why. I mean, look at this place," said Grant. "You got to figure we ain't the only ones that feel like that. I betcha everybody in this place's been down to that wagon tonight."

"Oh, I'm sure." Joseph took another healthy swallow.

"What do you think the attraction is?"

Joseph shrugged his massive shoulders. "Who the hell knows? Who cares? It's fun, that's all."

"Nah, there's gotta be more to it than that," said Chuck.

"What're you talking about?" Joseph asked the question with a kind of half-snarl.

"I don't know, for sure. I think it has something to do with how different that wagon is, you know. When I was lookin' in there tonight, it was like I was the only person in the world."

Dutton knew what Grant was talking about, but he wanted to hear someone else describe the experience, so he just nodded.

"You know, I picked up that gun and all of a sudden, it was like I was standin' out on this hill all by myself, and I couldn't hear any of the other guys shootin', or the crowd, or anything," said Grant in a soft, almost nostalgic tone of voice. "It was just me and all those faces hanging there in the dark. And when I started shootin' it was sorta like a . . . a *rhythm* I got into. Aim, shoot, and cock. Aim, shoot, and cock. It was like the most natural thing in the world, like I'd been doin' it all my life . . ."

"So?" Joseph was impressed with Chuck's primitive powers of description. Grant had touched upon some of the basic sensations that Dutton also had experienced.

"So? So don't you think that's kinda weird?"

Dutton shrugged and drank down another big swallow of beer. "Yeah, maybe it is. Maybe it ain't."

"Did you feel anything like I'm talkin' about?"

"What if I did?" Dutton wanted to know how far Chuck would take things. He wanted to know just how much of their experiences were exactly the same.

Grant nudged him. "Well, don't you think that's strange? Us both havin' the same feelings?"

"Not really. I think it has something to do with the display."

"Display? What the hell you mean, Joe?"

"This guy, Magister, must be using some kind of computer screens, you know . . . with lasers, or some kind of fancy new technology."

Even as he mouthed the words, Joseph was not certain he could even half-believe them, but he pressed on, just to see where it would take him. He was talking in a loud, authoritarian voice, the voice he used when he wanted to intimidate people into listening to him and, more important, agreeing with him.

"I seen stuff like that on television," he continued. "They can use these special colored lights and special shapes to almost hypnotize you, make you see stuff that isn't really there . . . make you feel like you've felt something, even when you really haven't. That's probably what this guy's got in that wagon. Just like them video games. Remember how weird everybody thought they were when old Tom first put them in here?"

Joseph had been getting so wrapped up in his lecture that he didn't realize that everybody around him had stopped talking to listen. When he paused to empty his mug, Joseph was more than a bit surprised to see half the bar on each side of him leaning in, staring at him. It was unsettling, and Dutton felt as though a spotlight had been suddenly turned on him, as though he were expected to continue his performance. He didn't know what else to say, and the silence was broken by one of the eavesdroppers.

"That's a pretty fair notion," said Red Lauterbach. "You're really somethin', ain't you, Mr. Dutton?"

"You really think that's what's goin' on?" Chuck put in.

Joseph took in a deep breath, expanding his chest like a cocky rooster. "Yeah, that's what I think."

"But why would that guy want to hypnotize people?" asked Bunky from behind the bar.

Joseph laughed to buy a little time while he figured out his response. "So you'll all want to come back the next night and put some more quarters in that damned jar, that's why!"

Some of the onlookers chuckled, but others retained serious expressions. The conversation had obviously touched upon a universal experience, and they wanted answers—if the town butcher was claiming he had them.

"I don't think that's all of it," said little Sam Havens as he lifted his Texaco cap just long enough to run his fingers through his greasy hair.

"What do you mean, Sam?" asked Cy Hartwell.

"Well, I think if Magister just wanted to make more money on us, he'd be chargin' more in the first place."

Several of the group nodded.

"Makes sense," said Chuck.

"Besides," Havens continued, "that thing's so much fun we don't have to be tricked into comin' back."

Dutton sneered. "You asshole . . . what I mean is that you're being hypnotized into *thinking* you're having fun, don't you see?"

Chuck Grant laughed, but the others remained silent. Havens glared at him for an instant, then started talking again.

"Nope. That can't be it. That ain't no video game we're lookin' at in the back of that wagon, and you know it."

"Maybe that guy's a magician," said Red Lauterbach.

"There's no such thing as magic," said Chuck. "It's all fake!"

"That's what I mean—maybe it's all fake shit . . ." Lauterbach scratched his scraggly red beard as everybody laughed.

Joseph signaled for another beer and Bunky moved to draw the brew into another frosted mug. The conversation was getting nowhere, and he just wanted to have another mug before making his way home. He was getting too drunk to think this hard, and to put it bluntly, he didn't give that much of a damn about that shooting gallery.

With the lull in the conversation, everybody else decided it would be a good time to call in some refills, and as Bunky ran back and forth behind the bar, the group of onlookers broke up and spread themselves out along the old polished mahogany slab. Only Sam Havens continued to look at Dutton. The little man slipped off his stool, circled Chuck Grant, and stationed himself at Dutton's other elbow.

"What is it, Sam?"

"Listen, there's somethin' else I think I oughta tell ya, Mr. Dutton . . ."

"Oh, yeah, what's that?"

Dutton didn't really want to hear any more from the likes of Havens, but the gas jockey had such an earnest look on his face that Joseph couldn't dismiss him.

"Well, tonight, when I was up at the counter shootin', and watchin' all them funny faces, I thought I saw somethin' really weird . . ."

Joseph sipped his beer, feeling a pleasant light-headed sensation slowly creep over him. "Oh, yeah, what'd you see?"

"Well, you know how them funny faces seem to change and kinda shift around in the dark? How the lights inside 'em make 'em look different all the time?"

"Yeah. Go on, get to the point, Havens."

"Well, for a minute there, for a second really, damned if I didn't see a face I knew in there!"

"What?" asked Chuck Grant.

"Who? Who did you see?" asked Joseph.

Havens grinned a little self-consciously. "Johannsen. I seen Johannsen's face in there. Just for a second, but I'd swear it was him."

"No shit?" said Chuck.

"No shit, I seen 'im."

"Now, why do you suppose you saw Johannsen in there?" asked Joseph.

"Who knows?" Havens grinned again. Then he lifted his cap and ran his fingers through his hair. "That guy's been here eight years and still can't speak no English worth a crap. He does know them car motors, though."

"You know, that's funny, Sam," said Chuck Grant. "I woulda never said nothin', but since you mentioned it—"

"What?" said Havens. "You seen 'im, too?"

Chuck rubbed his almost nonexistent chin with the back of his hand. "I don't know. I might have . . ."

"Ah, you two're crazy!" said Joseph. Here he was feeling pleasantly looped, and these two hayseeds were starting to get weird on him.

Sam ignored him. "Well, ain't that somethin'? What do you think about that? What do you think we oughta make outa all this?"

Dutton grabbed the little man by the shoulder and spun him around. He pushed his face right up into the splotchy, greasy countenance of Havens and snarled his best snarl.

"I'll tell you what *I* think, Havens," he said in a whispery voice. "I think we're making too much out of this whole thing already."

"You do?"

"It's just a carnival wagon, that's all. Right?"

"That's true," said Chuck Grant.

"And we're just out there having ourselves some fun," said Joseph. "There ain't nothing wrong with all of us having some fun, is there?"

Havens grinned. A little wider this time, and Joseph eased up on his grip on the smaller man's shoulder.

"Hell, no, Mr. Dutton. Just a little fun, that's all."

Dutton smiled, finished off the beer at the bottom of his mug. "And we shouldn't have to think about something as simple as having fun, should we?"

Havens chuckled this time, nodding his homely pin head. "You're right, Mr. Dutton. We don't have to think about nothin' if we don't want to!"

"How true, Sam. How true."

Dutton slapped Havens lightly on the back. It was a signal that their conversation was at an end, and Havens smiled again as he returned to his two friends on the other side of Chuck Grant.

"I think you're right, Joe," Grant said.

Joseph rubbed his belly as if to ease the beer more quickly along its appointed path. He chuckled and looked at his friend.

"I'm always right," he said.

CHAPTER 13

Magister watched the last of them scurry off to their vehicles. The party had ended for the moment, and they would go back to the warmth of their shelters still tingling with the excitement of the gallery. The light and laughter faded away, leaving him alone in the dark, comforting arms of the night. The feeble light of the moon cleansed him and he basked in its cool indifference.

As he moved to wipe the guns clean of the residue from their sweaty hands, he thought of how tightly they gripped the weapons, not realizing that he would soon hold them in a grip far tighter. It was far more difficult to wipe away the traces of his influence than it was to polish the dark metal of the guns. Once again, the mindless mechanism had been set into motion, and Magister smiled as he anticipated the terrible results.

He had stood among the group tonight, had felt the waves of emotion coming off them like convection currents. He could almost feed off their excitement, their heedless rush into the land of endless shadow, endless fear and loathing. These humans were a variegated lot—lots of juice and heat, lots of steam to run the engines of the night. He was a presence among them, but they did not seem to care or notice, so consumed were they by their own petty concerns and heaving emotions. He savored the heady mixture of their thoughts and feelings, and wondered how long the madness, once kicked into motion, would continue.

CHAPTER 14

Jamie had been sitting at breakfast when his mother got the phone call.

She didn't tell him what she had learned from the town's gossip network, but he could make his own logical deductions simply by paying attention and applying the powers of reasoning which Sherlock Holmes always championed.

When he saw that Mom had no intention of sharing her news with him, he decided not to press the issue. Sometimes adults felt that their kids should be sheltered from certain things. But usually their reasons for thinking like that were totally wrong.

Afterward, while he was pedaling his ten-speed to school, he pondered the real motivation for his mother's reticence, and could not come up with anything which made sense. As Mr. Spock would say, it was not logical.

The reality of what his mom had heard on the phone began to sink in, and Jamie knew that it was a significant event. He had his own ideas what it could mean, but he wanted to discuss them with Stella.

After all, Stella was his friend, maybe even his girlfriend.

This thought distracted him from his earlier, grimmer concerns, and he mentally replayed the kiss she'd given him yesterday. Just thinking about it made him feel dreamy.

He reached school early, as usual, and headed for the study hall to read comic books until the first bell.

Jamie knew he was bright, but he didn't flaunt it the way some of the other, more nerdy kids in his classes did. By keeping a lower profile, he was never singled out as a "smart fart" or a "brain" by the others. In fact, he was rather invisible to most of his classmates. They didn't persecute him because they didn't notice him.

It wasn't like he didn't have any friends at all, though. He did. But they were not close friends, and aside from some comradeship while they were actually in school, his classmates did not socialize with him.

There were a few neighborhood kids who came around to play ball or go exploring down by the railroad tracks and the stream, and sometimes they went to a movie. But that was about it. Jamie was pretty much a loner, but he didn't mind very much.

Since he had started getting to know Stella, however, things were different. He'd never really paid attention to stuff like the school dances or the Harvest Hayride, the plays or the Christmas Festival, but this year, he was wondering what it might be like to do those things with Stella.

The morning round of classes seemed to drag by with a surreal slowness, because he kept watching the clock. He had never anticipated lunch so much in

all his years of school. Just the thought of seeing
Stella was making him smile.

Man, you've got it bad, he told himself.

She was waiting for him outside the main doors to
the cafeteria, and she looked beautiful. Even indoors, the light danced and capered in her
strawberry-blond hair, and her complexion was so
clear and smooth that she looked like she was made
of porcelain. Stella wore a pair of beige corduroys
and a bulky purple and white striped sweater, making her look stylish and fashionable. Her clothes
always seemed so bright and colorful, and it made
him aware of his own outfit for the first time in his
life. What with his penchant for browns and grays
and plain old blue jeans, he must look very drab to
her.

"Hi, Jamie!" she said when she spied him splitting
off from the mob that surged into the dining area.
"What took you so long?"

He shrugged. "We had to clean up the table in
biology."

"What were you doing in there?"

"Today we started dissecting a frog."

Stella made a face. "God, right before lunch?
That's awful!"

Jamie smiled. "It's not so bad. There's no blood or
anything. They inject the veins with some kind of
rubbery stuff."

Stella squinched up her shoulders and made a face
like she was biting into a sour pickle. "It still sounds
gross."

"Yeah, maybe it is. I guess you just have to get
used to it."

"C'mon," she said, touching his arm. "Let's go sit down."

He followed her through the cafeteria line and then to a table in the corner of the hall where the rest of the tenth graders sat. They talked as they worked their way through the stuff on their trays, and gradually Stella worked the conversation around to her nightmare.

"It was really scary, Jamie. I never have nightmares without a good reason."

"Huh?" Sometimes she would say things like that and he wouldn't have the slightest idea what she was getting at.

"I mean, I know why I had that nightmare last night, Jamie . . ."

"Really?" Better to just let her explain it to him.

"I wrote some things in my journal about that carnival man, Mister Magister, right before I went to sleep. I don't trust him, Jamie. There's something not right about him." Stella looked sincere and intense as she stared at him with her sea-green eyes. They were so deep, Jamie felt like he could fall right into them.

"Maybe you're right, Stella."

"I know I'm right, Jamie. There's something different about the town ever since that shooting gallery showed up."

"Stella, did you hear about what happened this morning?"

Her expression changed from excitement to something close to fear. "No, I didn't hear anything. What're you talking about?"

"Somebody called my mom this morning while I was eating breakfast. She didn't tell me anything, but I could tell from what she was saying what had happened."

Stella reached across the table and took his hand. In spite of what he was about to tell her, her touch dispatched an electric shock through him. "Oh, Jamie, it's bad, isn't it? I can just tell from the look on your face."

"Yeah," he said. "Listen . . ."

CHAPTER 15

Six o'clock in the morning comes awful early, thought Sam Havens, especially if you've been bendin' your elbow too many times.

His old Camaro belched and farted its way down Center Street toward Wiggins' Texaco while Sam tried to get his mind unfogged. It was already quarter after, and ole Phil was probably gonna be pissed. Well, that was tough shit. A man has a right to have a little fun once in a while, even if it *is* on a work night. Yessireebob.

As he eased his wreck of a car into the station, he saw Phil Wiggins standing in the doorway to the office watching him come in. The most prominent feature of his boss was his front porch. Ole Phil had the original pot belly they named all them stoves after. And no matter what size shirts or pants he bought, it always seemed to bulge 'em out to the max.

Sam parked his car next to Phil's faded red pickup, paused to fire up a Marlboro, then climbed from behind the wheel.

"Sorry I'm late, boss . . ."

Wiggins harrumphed. "So what else is new? The one I'm worried about is Johannsen. That big Swede's never late."

"No kiddin'," said Sam, easing past his boss and into the office where he always kept the morning paper. "You give 'im a call over at Alice's?"

"Not yet. I figured I'd wait till you showed up, just in case he was riding in with you."

Now, that was funny, and Sam couldn't help from laughing. "Why in hell would I bring that big dummy into work with me? Christ, Phil . . ."

"I don't know. I don't know what to think." Phil picked up the telephone directory, thumbed through it till he found what he was looking for, then picked up the phone and punched in the number. It seemed like he waited a long time before anybody answered at the other end.

Sam sat back in the extra chair by the window and figured he'd just listen in.

"Morning, Alice, this is Phil Wiggins, did I wake you? . . . Well, I'm sorry about that, but I need you to check on something for me. Nils Johannsen ain't showed up for work yet, and that ain't like him at all . . . Right, so I was wondering if you knew if he'd left for work yet . . . Yeah, I know you were still asleep, but could you run upstairs and check to see if he's still there . . . ? Right. Good. Thanks, Alice." Phil covered the mouthpiece with his hand, looked at Sam, and shook his head. "That woman's meaner than catshit."

"What'd she say?" asked Sam.

"She's going upstairs to check on 'im. Probably overslept."

Sam nodded. Phil was more than likely right, but there was a funny feeling in the back of Sam's head that wanted to be saying that no, Phil probably wasn't right at all. It was like one of those pre-em-o-nitions Sam had heard about people having. He didn't really want to think about it, so he did his best to keep it out of his mind by picking up the morning paper.

Phil held on to the receiver. Alice must have gotten back on the line, because he listened for a bit before answering her: "Okay, Alice, you just wait right there, and I'll send Sam over to see what's going on . . . that's right, you just wait for him at the front door. Okay?"

Phil hung up the phone and looked at Sam.

"Well?"

"You heard me talking. Get your ass over to the boardinghouse."

"Jeez, what the hell for?" Normally, Sam would jump at the chance to get away from work, to run some silly little errand for Phil, but for some reason he could not explain, Sam didn't want to be running this particular errand this particular morning.

"'Cause I said so, that's why! Alice knocked on the boy's door and there warn't any answer, and she's scared to use her skeleton key."

"What the hell's she a-scared of?" Sam got up and ambled toward the door, slowlike.

"I don't know. You know how women are—says she's got a funny feeling about the whole thing."

Sam grinned and shook his head, but he knew exactly what that old bitch was talking about, because he was having the same kind of feeling.

But there was no getting out of this one, and he

figured he might as well get it over with. He lit another cigarette, started his Camaro, and headed up Center. He cut a right on Madison, then went down a block and made a left on Franklin. Alice Kirstin's rambling Victorian sat on the left side of the street, surrounded by big poplars and oaks.

The old bag was waiting for him on the front steps. She wore a bright pink and blue striped bathrobe, some kind of orange crocheted nightcap pulled down over her ears, and a pair of big fluffy green slippers. She looked like a circus clown that had forgotten to put on her makeup. But her expression looked anything but clownish. Alice looked kind of scared.

"Morning, Mrs. Kirstin," Sam said, putting a hand to his cap.

"Come on in here, Sam. He's on the top floor."

Sam followed her into the house, which was dark and dim because all the shades were still drawn tight. He had to wait a second or two while his eyes adjusted to the quick change from bright morning sun to this.

"I would have called Mr. Parker to help me, but he called last night and said he would be staying at some trollop's place, and old Mr. Vardeman, well, he's no help to anybody."

They were climbing the stairs now, and Sam had to hold on to the polished cherry banister because he still couldn't see clearly. They went up a second-floor hall and up another flight of narrow steps. There was another hallway up here with two doors off each side and an open bathroom at the opposite end.

"Here's his room," said Alice, stopping at the first door on the right.

Sam knocked.

No answer. It was quiet as a tomb in there. Damn, he wished he hadn't of thought of it like that.

He knocked again, this time really pounding. "Hey, Nils, you in there? It's Sam! Sam Havens . . . !"

He and Alice stood there for a minute and there was no response. She reached into her robe pocket and pulled out a brass ring of old keys.

"Here, Sam. This here one's the skeleton."

He took it and fitted it into the lock, and twisted it both directions. The lock snapped open with such ease that it almost startled him, and suddenly the door was swinging open. It didn't creak or anything.

As it slowly revealed the inside of the room, Sam felt the bottom of his stomach trying to make its way to the topside. He felt like his bowels were going to cut loose on him any second.

He didn't have to even walk into the room to see that something was wrong. The bed was still made like nobody'd touched it, and there was one of them funny-looking stands with a painted picture like you see artists with. It was propped up in the middle of the room and past the end of the bed.

"Go on in," said Alice, standing behind him.

Sam swallowed. He could feel his Adam's apple bob up and down real hard. He sucked in a breath and walked into the room, going only a few feet before he saw Johannsen's body sprawled out past the foot of the bed. He was lying on his back, clad in a plaid shirt and a pair of blue bib overalls. His glazed-over eyes stared up into eternity, and he held a long, thin paintbrush in his right hand.

"Oh, Jesus . . ." said Sam.

His stomach started flipping and flopping, and for

a minute he thought he might blow his breakfast. The alarm in the back of his head, the one he'd been trying to ignore, was clanging away now. It wasn't so much a noise in his head as it was a general state of panic that kept him from thinking straight. He took a couple of deep breaths and let them out slow and steady. What the hell was going on around here? He reached out to stop Alice, but she had seen it, too.

"Oh, no . . . Oh, no . . . this is awful. It's murder, Sam!" she whispered. "Somebody's killed him!"

"We don't know that for sure—"

"I better call Chief Nelson," she said.

"Yeah, I guess so," said Sam.

"Don't touch anything!" she said, grabbing his arm and squeezing it. "That's what they always say on television, so it must be right!"

"Yeah, right." He couldn't stop staring at the body, at those big buggy eyes staring up like he'd been shocked to realize that he was checking out.

"You stay here and keep an eye on things till I get back," said Alice. Then she disappeared behind him and was scurrying down the steps to the telephone in the first-floor foyer.

Sam didn't want to stay there, but he guessed he had no choice till the police showed up. Chief Nelson would want to be getting "statements," more than likely. That was the way they did it on TV. Sam had never seen a dead body outside of a funeral home, and his natural curiosity began to get the best of him. He inched farther into the room, being careful not to disturb anything.

The first thing he noticed was that there was hardly any color in Johannsen's face. It was almost a chalky white, tinged with the suggestion of blue, and his skin didn't even look real. He'd always been on the pale side, but this was ridiculous. Looking up to the easel, Sam saw a piece of canvas stretched out on a wood frame. He didn't know anything about that kind of stuff, but the half-finished picture looked pretty nice to him. He figured that Johannsen had been painting on it when he died.

Now, that was sure funny. A big, silly-looking guy like Nils—you would have never figured him to be into something faggoty like painting pictures. Sam shrugged as he looked around the room and saw all the other finished pictures hung all over the walls. It just goes to show you never know about people.

CHAPTER 16

Stella felt like she'd been stabbed through the heart with an icicle.

The coldness spread out from the center of her chest, like an ever-growing stain. It seeped into her arms and legs, and for an instant, she thought she was dying.

"Oh, Jamie . . . don't you see what's happening here?"

His face was a tight-lipped mask as he looked at her. After a moment's hesitation, he nodded slowly. "I think I do. I see what this all looks like, but I don't want to jump to any conclusions yet."

"What?" She squeezed his hand even tighter.

"You're going to tell me that Magister's behind all this, right?"

"You know he is!" she almost shouted, and had to be careful not to get any of the other kids' attention. She waited until the general din of the cafeteria swarmed over them like a cloud of bees.

Jamie half-grinned, but the smile faded quickly. "Well, Stella, I don't know it—but I do suspect him. Still, we've got to go about this rationally, like detectives. Or scientists, even. We need to gather some facts."

"Jamie, here're your facts: A strange guy all dressed in black shows up with a weird shooting gallery, and two days later, two people in our town are dead!"

"Yeah, okay, go on," he said.

"Go on? That's all there is to tell. That's all you need!" she whispered at him harshly, hoping that he would understand that she wasn't angry with him, just excited.

"No, it's not, Stella. It's just what they call circumstantial evidence."

"That Mister Magister killed them, and you know it." Stella's heart was racing in her breast, and her breathing was getting labored. She had never felt so worked up just sitting at a table and talking.

"Okay, okay." Jamie held up his hands like he was surrendering. "Okay, Stella, let's say that Magister did kill Clarence Williams and Mr. Johannsen —what about his motive?"

"His *what*?"

"We have to try to figure out why he killed them. I mean, even if he did kill them, what good does it do him? What's he getting out of it?"

"Why do we need to know his motivation?" Stella knew that Jamie meant well, but he seemed to be getting wrapped up in the purely rational end of the situation.

"Because then we might be able to predict what his next move will be. And then maybe we can prevent anybody else from getting killed." Jamie spoke slowly and carefully.

He was right, she realized, but she was also right. This was not something he could just deduce like

Sherlock Holmes; it was something she could feel in the deepest part of her being.

"All right, I see what you mean," she said after a pause. "But what should we do next? I was thinking that maybe we should go see Chief Nelson."

Jamie shook his head. "With what? I mean, what are we going to tell him? We've got to have some proof."

Stella nodded, but said nothing. She knew Jamie was right again, but she couldn't fight the feeling that he was trying too hard to refute whatever ideas she offered. Maybe she should try a different tack.

"Okay, Jamie, let's try to put down whatever facts we know." She pulled a piece of paper from one of her school notebooks, and readied her ballpoint pen. "First off, how do you know your information is correct?"

He grinned. "I don't for sure. Dr. Finlay had to go over to the boardinghouse early this morning. He's the town coroner, when he has to be. And Doc Finlay's nurse, Mrs. Schallert, is my mom's best friend. And that's who called this morning."

"But *you* weren't on the phone. How do you know exactly what she said?"

"I could tell some of it by the things my mother was saying—you know, by logical deduction." Jamie smiled, and it was a very charming smile. "And in the second place Mrs. Schallert talks so loud that my mom has to hold the phone away from her ear. Anybody in the room can hear what she's saying."

Stella giggled as she conjured up the image, then composed herself as she prepared to write. "Okay, so let's go over it one more time."

"Now, let's see . . . there was no apparent cause of death and the doc's going to have to do an autopsy. That means that if it was murder, there was no immediate sign of violence. Also, the bed hadn't been slept in, and the body appeared to have been dead since the previous night." Jamie paused and looked at her. "Now, what does that tell you?"

Stella didn't answer right away. Jamie was obviously asking her to think logically, and she didn't want to disappoint him. He had such long eyelashes, it was incredible. She knew lots of girls who would kill to have lashes like that.

"Well?" he prompted.

"I was thinking. Give me a break! Well, I guess it would depend upon the exact time Mr. Johannsen died, wouldn't it? I mean, if they figure that when he died, Magister was seen down at his gallery, then it doesn't seem possible that Magister could have killed him, right?"

"That's exactly right, Stella. You might make a good detective one of these days."

"No thanks, I'd rather be a writer."

"I know. Just kidding. But really, the time of death is very important to our case," he said. "I'll keep my ears open and see what I can find out."

She looked down at her paper. "Anything else we know for sure?"

He shrugged. "Not really. I guess it's safe to assume that neither of the victims had any terminal illnesses, but that's about all I can think of. If Dr. Finlay can't come up with a cause of death, then we have one more fact: Both people died for no apparent reason and no known cause."

Stella felt a shudder pass through her as he finished talking. In spite of the bright lights and the noise of the cafeteria, she suddenly felt quite alone. Even having Jamie right across the table from her could not dispel her sudden sensation of complete isolation.

"That's pretty scary, Jamie."

He took her hand in his, held it tightly. "Yeah, I know."

"What else can we do?"

"I don't know."

"I think we should go down to Harker's meadow tonight."

Jamie seemed somewhat surprised. "Really?"

"Yes. I want to see what's going on down there, and I want to see this Magister for myself."

"That sounds good to me," said Jamie. "Want to ride our bikes?"

"That's probably the best idea. But I don't have a light on mine if it gets too dark."

"As long as you have reflectors and you ride facing the traffic, you should be okay."

"I don't think I have reflectors either."

"Well, I do." He smiled. "So you'll just have to ride behind me, okay?"

She smiled and nodded. He sounded so protective and full of concern. It was interesting to listen to Jamie talk. Sometimes he sounded mature and wise, and at other times he sounded just like the teenager that he was. It made Stella think of what an awkward age they were struggling with. It was time to throw off the things of childhood and take up the trappings of the adult world. But this was a middle period, a twilight zone where the issues and choices and expectations were not clear, and you didn't know how to act or what to say, or even how to say it. She was thankful that she had found somebody as sincere and understanding as Jamie. He would make the passage a lot more tolerable.

Suddenly the sound of the school bell cut through the cacophony of the dining hall. Chairs were pushed back from the tables as everyone prepared to dump their trays and return to the classrooms. Stella stood up as Jamie joined her.

"Can you walk home with me after class?" she asked.

He frowned, looked down at his shoes for a moment. "Sorry, I can't. I have a meeting with my biology teacher about this year's County Science Fair. I've got a pretty neat project planned, and I have to see him about it."

She understood and smiled her best smile for him. "That's okay. I should go right home and get my homework done anyway if we're going down to the meadow tonight."

"Yeah," he said. "If I walk home with you, we'll burn off lots of time talking."

"Nothing wrong with that," said Stella, giggling to break the light film of tension she felt taking shape.

"You're right about that."

The crowd surged past and around them.

"We'd better get going," she said. "See you tonight. Around seven okay?"

"Yeah. I'll come to your house."

"Okay. Bye."

He nodded and disappeared into the stream of kids filing through the cafeteria doors. She picked up their trays and took them over to the dead-stack, then slipped into the flow herself.

It was going to be a long, long afternoon.

Aunt Leah was downstairs getting dinner ready while Stella finished her homework. She hated doing her assignments right after class because it made the school day seem like it went on forever. But tonight it was for a good cause. It was exciting to be investigating Mister Magister's Magnificent Gallery, but there was also the possibility of danger, and Stella was worried.

Should they be doing this kind of snooping around without anyone else knowing? Suppose Magister was some kind of escaped lunatic? A child killer or ax murderer?

No, that was silly. A crazy wouldn't have the resources or the time to establish such an elaborate disguise.

But suppose he somehow discovered that she and Jamie suspected him of the deaths? What would he do? Would they be in any danger themselves? Could he kill them, too?

Of course he could.

Then why were they planning all this? It wasn't a game they were playing. It was real, and there was a possibility that one or both of them could die.

She thought of calling Jamie and voicing her fears. She hoped he would tell her it was just her imagination running at double time. She was probably reading too much into the whole thing. Maybe. Was it possible that the two deaths and the carnival man's appearance were just coincidences?

No. It couldn't be.

Stella was certain of that. But if it was so obvious to her that Magister and the deaths were somehow connected, how come no one else in the town seemed to notice, or care?

She closed her notebook and set it on the desk. She needed to get her mind off the whole issue for a little while. Moving across the room, she turned on the small television on her dresser. She hardly ever actually sat down and watched it, but she often turned it on when she was bored or restless or even feeling lonely. For some reason having a TV on made her feel not quite as alone.

Sitting on the edge of her bed, she let herself get lost in the lyrics and bizarre images of a rock video. A young blond girl was running down an alley in a big city at night, and a band of weird-looking guys were chasing her. The music was hard and fast and full of danger. One of the guys grabbed her and she immediately started rubbing herself against him. Stella did not really like what she was watching, but there was definitely an odd fascination to the stylized, symbolic violence and sexuality of the video.

Many of the music videos were like that, and Stella figured her reaction to them was wrapped up in her recent interest in sex and love.

The images on the screen faded and changed. A new video took shape. Several lines of white letters in the left corner of the screen identified title, artist, and label. A boy and girl stood atop a desert dune at sunset. He held her in his arms and kissed her while a hot wind lifted and fluttered their billowy clothes and long hair. The music swelled to a crescendo. She thought of Jamie and how she would like him to kiss her like that, of how it would feel to be so totally alone somewhere that they could do whatever they wanted.

The thought excited her and, at the same time, frightened her. It seemed that she was reeling forward into darkness, into a region of so many unknowns that she would never be able to make sense of any of it. At times it seemed like such a twisted mass of facts, full of so many mysteries, that it would all overwhelm her.

But she would not let it. Especially with Jamie right alongside. He gave her strength and inspiration.

"Stella! Time to eat!"

"I'll be right down," she called. She switched off the TV, exited her room, and descended the stairs.

"What were you doing up there all afternoon?" asked Aunt Leah.

"I did my homework early because Jamie and I are going to ride out to the meadow and see the carnival wagon." Stella took her seat at the table and hoped her aunt would approve of her plans.

"You, too?" Aunt Leah smiled as she sat down and started dishing out the vegetables. "You know, all the teachers at school were talking about that wagon today! Some kind of shooting gallery, isn't it?"

"Yes, that's what I heard."

"Ann Mulligan wants me to ride out there with her."

Stella was a bit surprised, but tried to conceal it. "Really? Are you going?"

"I think so. She said she'd pick me up around eight." Leah paused to sip her tea. "You could go out with us, if you'd like."

"No, I already told Jamie I'd go with him, if that's okay with you, that is."

Aunt Leah smiled. "Of course, dear. Just be careful, that's all."

"I will."

"You really seem to get along with this Rodin boy, don't you?"

Stella grinned, and tried to concentrate on her food. Why did she suddenly feel defensive and embarrassed—just because the talk concerned Jamie?

"Well, so far, I do, yes," she said finally.

"He seems like a nice boy."

Stella listened while her aunt reminisced about her first real boyfriend, and then gently steered the conversation to other things. Inwardly, she was more than mildly surprised that her aunt would be going out to see the shooting gallery. The attraction seemed to be affecting everybody.

Finally, dinner was over. Stella helped her aunt clean up the kitchen. Just as they were finishing, Jamie appeared on the front porch.

The sun was westering in the sky, sending out smears of warm color. It was a beautiful autumn evening, just cool enough for a sweater or a light jacket. It was hard to believe that the coming winter would change everything so quickly. Fall was such a perfect time of the year; Stella wished it would always stay like it was tonight.

Stella pedaled behind Jamie as they headed for the intersection of Church Lane and Center Street. They passed the picket fences and hedges which divided the lawns and properties of the shaded back street. All the houses were neat and clean and orderly. Shutters freshly painted and the gingerbread all gleaming white; everyone had finished getting ready for the rough weather. Brampton seemed to be such a nice place to live. So quiet and well kept, it was hard to believe that anything could be actually wrong here.

She needed to know if Jamie thought they were in

any real danger; she asked him when they reached the traffic light at Center.

"No, I don't think so," he said. "Unless you think this guy Magister has some kind of special powers."

"Powers? Like what?"

He shrugged. "Oh, I don't know. Something supernatural."

She looked at him, and from his expression, she could tell that as a young scientist, he did not allow himself any beliefs in such mystical claptrap.

"Jamie, I'm surprised that you would even mention something like that."

"Well, to be honest, I said it for your benefit. That kind of stuff never made much sense to me. But some people think it's possible."

"He might be a murderer," said Stella.

Jamie shrugged. "There's nothing supernatural about that."

"But if he is, doesn't that put us in danger?"

"Gee, Stella, I don't see how we'd be in any more danger than anybody else in town. I mean, there's no way he can know we're on to him. As far as he's concerned, we're just a couple of kids, right?"

She nodded, but said nothing.

"Well, come on," he said, pushing off and heading east on Center Street.

She followed him. They rode on the left, facing the traffic. There weren't many cars coming that way. All the vehicles seemed to be heading out of Brampton, toward the meadow.

"Hey!" cried Jamie. "Look at that, will you?"

Lines of cars stretched up the state highway on both shoulders. Stella had never seen it more crowded—not even for the regular carnival. It

looked like half the town was already out there, and
the other half was on the way. It was crazy, absolute-
ly crazy. How could one silly little wagon cause such
a stir in everybody?

Jamie pedaled past the long line of parked cars,
and Stella followed closely behind him. They actually went past the meadow and the wagon, then
slipped between two cars and coasted to a stop in the
alfalfa grass.

"Lots of people already here," Jamie said, looking
at the panorama spread out before them.

Stella nodded as she took in the scene. Someone,
maybe old man Harker himself, had strung up
colored lights in the trees, and there was a portable
hot-dog stand steaming into the crisp autumn night.
People had brought picnic dinners and jugs of hot
coffee. They stood in little talkative circles or sat in
folding chairs and discussed the excitement of the
evening. Stella was truly amazed by it all. In just a
few days, something had happened to everybody,
but she couldn't be sure what it was.

"Okay, we're here," said Jamie. "Let's go . . ."

Stella chained her bike to a sapling maple and
followed Jamie as he walked slowly toward the
crowd. Stella caught glimpses of cliques from high
school. Over by the lights and the lemonade stand,
Marcia, Suzanne, and Kelley huddled together, giggling and talking in exaggerated whispers. A large
clot of boys from the eleventh grade hung about the
wagon like a swarm of insects. Stella sensed a
difference in people this night. There was a feeling
of . . . of surliness—yes, that was it—which seemed
to radiate from most of them.

Continuing to scan the crowd, her gaze went

beyond the familiar faces and into the soft shadows of the trees behind the wagon. There she saw the pale face, the gaunt, almost sunken features of the attraction's proprietor. Only the man's eyes seemed to be alive, and they shined in his head like polished pieces of the night. Mister Magister's black cape embraced him like a dark lover, almost completely obscuring clothes that seemed ill-fitting and uncomfortable. He looked like a wax figure as he stood in the wings of the little theater he had created. Nothing moved save his eyes.

For an instant, their gazes locked and Stella was staring into the depths of his eyes, like holes into his skull, and she could feel him penetrating her head, violating her innermost thoughts. It was an ugly, dirty sensation, yet it was compelling and hypnotic. A part of her wanted him to stare into her secret self forever. It was a sensual, almost sexual thing, and she had to force herself to look away.

A coldness seeped out of her as the contact was broken. Risking a final, quick look back at the man, Stella felt something like disappointment when she saw that his gaze was elsewhere.

She felt used. It made her think about what Jamie had said, and she knew there were parts of the world which did not, and could not, fall neatly into his little compartmentalized, scientific boxes. Whatever had just passed between her and Magister was surely one of these things, and she wondered if she could ever make Jamie recognize or understand such a thing.

She felt a tug at the sleeve of her sweater, and looked to see him smiling at her.

"Hey, you okay?" asked Jamie.

"Yes, I'm sorry . . ."

"You looked pretty spacey there for a minute. What happened?"

"Mister Magister. He was looking at me. I felt weird."

Jamie nodded. "Yeah, it's all part of the act. I've been watching him myself. Real theatrical, don't you think? With all that black, and the hat. And he doesn't pitch like most carnies do. He's real cool about it."

"There's more to it than that," said Stella.

Jamie nodded as he looked through the crowd. "Well, let's go take a look at the shooting gallery. That's what we're here for, right?"

Stella nodded, but could not speak. She was disappointed in Jamie. Not that it was really his fault, but she could tell that he was not feeling the difference out here. He was not attuned to what she could only call the absolute strangeness of Magister and his Magnificent Gallery. People just shouldn't be so enthralled with something this simple. What should be a distraction, a diversion at best, seemed to have become almost an obsession with them. She paused to listen to snippets of the conversations which chittered and flitted all about them. *The targets. The guns. The gallery.* It was all they could talk about.

Couldn't any of them look at Magister and know there was something wrong?

Was she the only one?

Stella fought off another chill and followed Jamie toward the gallery.

CHAPTER 17

"Til! Aren't you ready yet?" cried Joanna from the downstairs foyer. "What's taking you so long?"

"I'll be right down, honey!"

Tilden Strong stood before the bathroom mirror, studying the sagging mask of his face. He kept telling himself that he was only going back to the meadow because his wife and daughter had been caught up in the atmosphere which surrounded the shooting gallery.

He was only going out there to please the two of them.

Right. What bullshit that was.

Couldn't he even be honest with himself?

Sooner or later, he knew that he must. But God, he wished he could talk to somebody about what he'd seen, what he knew . . .

He had no idea of how things were happening, the actual mechanics of the process, but he damned well knew there was a cause-and-effect relationship. As to why or how or any of the other questions, he had no answers. And he knew he should do something about it—but he felt weak, afraid.

This would be the third straight night out there, and when he stepped up to the counter this evening, he wondered whose face he would see.

Chop! Chop!

Joseph Dutton whacked at the pork loin with the easy swing of a long-practiced hand. The cleaver came down with a smooth, silky stroke, slicing through the bright red meat with a clean *snick,* punctuated by a solid *thunk.* He often stood by his butcher's block and fantasized other things beneath the cleaver's blade.

There were so many jerks in the world, and so many of them seemed to live right in this town. But he got them all sooner or later beneath his fantasy blade, cutting off—or out—the offending part. Hands for stealing, tongues for wise-mouthing, eyes for looking where they shouldn't, and even a few dongs for getting stiff in places they shouldn't.

He'd stopped worrying about Millie years ago. Ever since that night he'd dragged her down into the basement, where he kept his grinding and sharpening tools, and told her he'd cut her heart right out if he ever caught her fooling around, he knew she'd been too scared to try anything.

Besides, he was a big man. He kept her plenty satisfied. Whenever he wanted it, he just flopped her down on that bed and pounded her like a tent peg. Wham-bam-thank-you-ma'am.

He grinned as he finished dressing the chops and wrapped them in white, waxy paper. He wrote Mrs. Holliday's name across the back with a felt-tipped pen, then tossed the package into the cold-cabinet.

Dutton nodded to himself as he returned to his punitive fantasies. He knew there was nothing wrong with that kind of thinking. Didn't all those A-rab countries do that stuff? You shit around over there and they cut something off. That's the way it should be over here too—if you're dumb enough to get caught.

He chuckled and checked the list taped to the side of the cold-cabinet. That was the last of the special orders for tomorrow morning, and now he could clean himself up and get out of the damned shop. Oh, sure, it kept a roof over his head and all that shit, and he had been able to salt away some money for retirement, but he hated his job as surely as he hated his wife and his kids. He kept telling himself that he should love them, but damn, they'd been nothing but millstones around his neck for so many years.

Sometimes he would think about all the adventuring he could have done if he'd just stayed in the navy and let his uncle take care of him for the rest of his life. Well, it might be too late for that kind of stuff, but he still knew how to have himself some fun.

Time to get washed up and roll on down to the gallery. He loved that shooting gallery like he never took to one of those games before. There was something about this one that was something like pussy. He grinned as he considered his clever simile. You just kept coming back for more. You just could never get enough of it. Yeah, it was time to go shoot a few rounds, then maybe stop off at Donnegan's and wet the old whistle.

Joseph Dutton smiled as he wiped his hands on his apron. Sometimes life was just right.

Jack Nelson hated eating at the Express Diner. But every third night, he took the evening shift to give his officers a break, and the cheapest food in town was at the Express, so what was a man going to do? He turned on his beeper so that if anybody called the station and left a message on the machine, he could call in and still respond. He loved all the new electronic gadgets they were coming up with these days.

He bought one of those supersonic bug 'n' pest chasers, and he had a remote control on his garage door, and he just got a little widget to stick on his key ring that beeped real loud if he clapped his hands. Follow the beep, and *bingo*, he found his keys. It was a great gadget, just like that phone-answering rig with the pocket beeper. It really helped keep his job as the town's police chief from getting too complicated.

Sliding onto a stool at the counter, he noticed that the place was practically empty. There was a truck driver down at the opposite end, probably on his way into Des Moines, shoveling in the blue-plate special. But aside from him and Josie, the Express was deserted.

"Hiya, Chief," said Josie, who looked like she was putting on the pounds faster than her hair was turning gray. It was amazing how fast a woman started to fall apart. Hit that menopause thing, and *bingo*, they'd had it. Men, they seemed to hang on better.

"Evening, Josie. Where the H is everybody? Down to Harker's meadow again?"

"I figure," said the waitress/short-order cook. "Everybody that's been in here tonight was talking about it."

Jack Nelson sighed. "Yeah, all my men have got that gallery on their brains, too."

"You'd think that with all the chance they get to target-shoot with their real guns, they wouldn't care about that toy stuff," said Josie, sticking the menu under his steepled hands.

Jack grinned. "Well, I been down there myself, and I'll tell you, the setup that carnie's got is better than anything I've ever seen. I couldn't keep from shooting in there myself!"

"No kiddin'?"

"It's the truth, darlin'. Matter of fact, I might amble on up to the meadow a little later myself."

Josie poured him a cup of his usual coffee. "Ain't you on duty tonight?"

"Yeah, but there's nothing going on. Nothing ever goes on in Brampton except some of the high school kids acting up, and they're probably all out to the meadow these nights."

"What about them two people dyin' like that?" asked Josie. "I thought that was kinda somethin'."

The Chief shook his head. "Nah, just one of those weird coincidences, I figure. Nothing to get psyched up about, that's what I say."

"Yeah, I guess you're right," Josie said, pulling out her order pad. "So what'll it be, Chief?"

Four years ago, when Gary Needham observed that there wasn't a computer and software outlet within fifty miles of Brampton, he took it as a sign of potential success for the shrewd entrepreneur. He opened up Mr. Chips' Computers & Software Center, and business immediately boomed. He was convinced he had walked into a gold mine.

But he wasn't so sure anymore. After all the just plain folk had bought machines, they discovered something Gary didn't want them to know: They really didn't have much use for the home computer, other than reconciling checkbooks, keeping recipes, or playing Pac Man. In fact, most people found that it was easier to not bother reconciling their checking account statements and to keep their recipes in an old tin index-card box. And of course, eventually everyone got sick of Pac Man . . .

Now, after the boom had turned to bust, Gary was hanging on to his business by his fingernails. He was supported by a small contingent of local businessmen and farmers who had computerized their operations, plus a bunch of school kids who wanted to see the latest interactive-adventure games on the Softsel best-seller list.

Gary was convinced that the "micro age" would eventually take hold even in places like Brampton, but it was going to be a slower process than the first novelty boom had indicated. He had stopped thinking about retiring at the age of forty—now only six years in the future—and had faced the reality of scraping along in his business like the rest of the hardscrabble businessmen in the area.

He checked his watch and saw that it was almost six P.M., which meant that he could close his empty store and get down to the meadow for a little relaxation before going home to the empty house. When Angie discovered that she had not married the next instant millionaire, and that the store was going to mean hard work and sacrifice, she had packed up and taken off to sponge off her sister in Los Angeles.

Now separated and footing the bills alone, Gary wasn't all that crazy about going home to the stripped-down house that wasn't warm and inviting anymore. He welcomed the small measure of excitement that the traveling shooting gallery had brought to him. It actually gave him something to look forward to at the end of each day.

His therapist at the mental health clinic in Garrison would have probably told him that the shooting gallery was providing him with an outlet for all the pent-up hostility and aggression he was feeling toward Angie. And maybe that wasn't just a lot of who-struck-john.

Gary had thought of his ex-wife's face more than once while he peered into that wonderful darkness where the funny faces bobbed and weaved and changed.

Bang, honey . . . you're dead.

Georgiana Finch adjusted the flame under the pot roast and checked the watch over the stove. Another hour and Peter would be home. She could get the kids in from playing, they could eat a quick dinner, and then she could get out of the house for a few hours.

It wasn't like the house was a prison or anything like that, but she did start to feel confined as fall started to come on. It meant that winter was on its way with all the blistering cold weather—and then she would be indoors even more than now.

Thank goodness for that shooting gallery. Ever since it arrived, she felt like she had something extra in her life, something with a little mystery and excitement. Her husband had needed to convince her to take a turn at the counter the first night the family stopped at Harker's meadow, but once she had felt the weight and power of that gun in her hands, Georgiana was forever grateful. Standing there eyeing up those targets gave her a sensation of . . . what was it? Accomplishment and power. It was a combination of feelings never felt by her before, and she liked it.

But it wasn't that she disliked being a housewife. She and Peter had decided that kids were better off being supervised by their mother than by baby-sitters and day-care center employees. Especially with all this talk in the news recently about child molesters and missing children.

Just the thought of people like that out in the world made her upset.

If Georgiana ever caught anybody planning to do something like that to Justin or Jeanette, and she had a gun like that one at the gallery, she wouldn't think twice about shooting them right between their beady, perverted little eyes.

That would fix them good.

CHAPTER 18

"Stella Chambers . . ." said a slippery-sounding voice from behind her. A pudgy finger briefly touched the back of her shoulder before she moved away from it.

Quickly turning, she encountered a large, florid-faced man wearing a poplin jacket over a sloppy shirt and an ill-fitting pair of trousers. He was looking at her with a leering, out-of-kilter grin and eyes that kept flicking up and down her body as if to strip her naked as she stood there. He stared at her with a bald fascination, which would have made her very uncomfortable if it had not angered her first.

"Hello, Mr. Dutton. Can I help you with anything?"

He smiled as he pulled a thick, ropy cigar from his jacket pocket, stuck it between his teeth. "Not really. I was just noticin' that you sure are growin' up in a hurry . . . Goin' to be a beautiful woman one of these days, Stella."

"Thank you, Mr. Dutton," she said icily.

What should have been a compliment to make her

156

blush only angered her more because he made no effort to conceal the obvious lust in his words and gaze. She had never respected Mr. Dutton, but had never been able to pinpoint the reason for her feelings. Now, as she was growing older, the true character of the man was coming clear to her, and she was glad to know that her instincts had been correct.

"You come out for a little fun?" he asked, oblivious to her coolness.

"No, I just stopped by to see what's got the whole town so mesmerized."

"Mesmerized!" He chuckled, then paused to light his cigar. For a moment his jowled face was obscured by a great blue cloud. "Now, that's a fancy word to be usin' around us simple folks!"

"Sorry." She looked around for Jamie, wishing that he would join her. With Jamie present, she would feel more confident in dealing with Mr. Dutton. Where had he gotten off to? One second they were walking along, she following him, and then she had been distracted by the town butcher. Nervously, her gaze searched in vain through the crowd.

"Looking for somebody?" asked Dutton.

"My boyfriend," she said, surprising herself. It was the first time she had ever called Jamie that, and it felt good rolling off her tongue.

"Boyfriend, eh? Yeah, I'd figure a girl like you would have plenty of bucks licking around her."

Stella glared at him. "You have such a way with words, Mr. Dutton."

He grinned unevenly. "Why, thank you."

Stella decided to take the offensive.

"You never answered my question, Mr. Dutton."

"And what was that?"

"What's the attraction out here? How come everybody's so excited about a dinky little shooting gallery?"

Dutton's eyebrows tilted toward one another. He looked at her sternly. "Listen, young lady, that thing's one hell of a contraption. You ain't tried it, you wouldn't know. It's more fun than most of the women in this town, you can take my word for it!"

"But *why*, Mr. Dutton? That's what I'd like to know."

He looked at her for a moment, puffed on his cigar, and blew out the smoke through a scowl. "What the hell's goin' on here? You workin' for the newspaper or somethin'? Fun's fun, that's all! It ain't no big deal! There ain't nothin' to it, believe me."

"Really?" she said as she sensed his defensiveness building. Now it was her turn to grin slyly. It was interesting to see how the penetrating lance of intellect and reason could deflate even the largest balloons of arrogance and stupidity.

"Yeah, now if you'd just excuse me, I'm goin' to have me some *fun*. Ain't no crime in that, is there?"

Stella smiled. "Not that I know of. But I'm young yet . . ."

She watched him wheel away from her and lumber up to the wagon. A trio of junior high school boys were shooting into the darkness when Dutton approached. Dropping a quarter into the almost-full Mason jar, he assailed the closest boy, wrenching the rifle from his hands.

"Hey, I wasn't finished yet!" The boy's face twisted into instant hatred.

"Oh, yes, you was," said Dutton, ignoring him as he leaned on the counter and drew a bead upon the first target.

"That's not fair!" cried the boy. He looked to his friends and out into the crowd for support, but everyone seemed to be ignoring him.

Dutton paused in his shooting and looked down at him. Stella found the butcher's face to be a study in malevolence. "Listen, boy . . ." said Dutton as sweat popped from his pores despite the cool night breeze. "There ain't nothin' in this life that's fair! It's about time you learned that."

Then turning back to the gallery, Dutton dismissed him. The boy cowered away and melted into the crowd.

Stella looked about to see everyone's reaction to the nasty little scene, but no one had seemed to notice.

Or maybe it was something else, she thought, as she walked through the crowd looking for Jamie. Maybe they don't care.

CHAPTER 19

He wasn't sure how it happened, but one minute Stella was following him and then, when he turned around to say something to her, she wasn't there. He had wormed his way pretty close to the front of the gallery, and the people were all elbow-to-elbow right there as they cheerfully eased closer to the counter.

But where was Stella?

Suddenly there was a force moving through the crowd, pushing everyone to one side or the other. It was a tidal surge, a rippling effect, like a large stone tossed into a calm pool. Jamie looked over his shoulder to see the town butcher cutting a swath through the crowd and bullying his way to the gallery's counter.

Jamie shook his head as he watched Mr. Dutton yank a rifle from Emory Heywood's hands. Emory was a pretty hefty kid, but he was no match for Dutton.

What a jerk, thought Jamie. And everybody was going to let him get away with it, too.

Turning away from the incident, feeling guilty that

he himself did not have the nerve to stand up to Mr. Dutton, Jamie resumed his search for Stella.

As Jamie scanned the crowd for her, he felt somebody tugging at his sleeve. Distracted, he looked to the left and saw Steve Yeager with Spunky Maddox. They were both from his science classes. Jamie would not really consider them close friends, but they seemed to get along with him at school, and Steve was his lab partner in biology.

"Hey, Rodent, how're you doin'?" asked Steve with a lopsided grin. "You been up to shoot yet?"

"Nah, I just got here," Jamie said, his gaze still darting about, trying to locate Stella.

"So did we," said Spunky, who was short and slightly overweight. "You wanna take some shots with us?"

Jamie hesitated. "I don't know. I'm here with somebody else."

He didn't want to tell them it was a girl, that it was Stella. He didn't know how they would react and he didn't feel like dealing with these guys if they were going to razz him about it.

"Hey, that don't matter," said Spunky. "You're just here to shoot anyway, right?"

"Well, not exactly." But Steve and Spunky weren't really listening as they jostled forward toward the counter. The crowd seemed to sense when someone had given up their place at the counter and would surge forward to fill the empty spaces. Jamie felt himself being carried along with the other two boys. It was as much a mental process as a physical one, and that bothered him.

"Come on, Rodent. We're gettin' closer to the front," said Steve Yeager. He grabbed Jamie's jacket and tugged him along.

For an instant, as he continued to scan the crowd for Stella, he caught a flash of her yellow sweater. She had just turned away from Mr. Dutton, and was moving away from the gallery. As she headed back into the thickest part of the crowd, he lost sight of her.

"Wait!" he said to Steve, looking back at him for an instant. When he turned again and called out Stella's name, she had disappeared.

"Come on, Jamie," said Steve Yeager. "It's almost our turn! Look how close we are."

Confused, he felt pulled in two directions. The closer he was drawn to the gallery, the more strongly he felt its influence, its powerful attraction. The unearthly force combined with the insistent voices of his friends who wished for him to join in their adventure.

And that was a good word for it—adventure. He was definitely on an exploratory mission. He really should find Stella first, but with the crowd so big, this might be the only time he would get to the counter. Stella was close by. She would find him eventually. It wasn't like they were lost or anything like that.

"You comin'?" asked Spunky.

Jamie nodded and moved up to the final rank before the counter. Mr. Dutton and two younger boys were sighting down the barrels of their rifles, and as Jamie drew closer to the counter, he could almost look over the shooters' shoulders.

But not quite.

He could see nothing of the gallery itself, and this intrigued him even more. Suddenly, he found himself anxious and wanting to get up to the counter. Without thinking, his right hand was in his jeans pocket fishing out a quarter.

He did notice one thing, however, and that was the intensity of the people shooting. They all seemed totally engrossed with what they were doing. It didn't look carefree, like regular old fun.

And yet everyone was consumed by it.

Finally the boys lay down their rifles, and a moment later Mr. Dutton followed their lead. As they stepped away from the counter, Jamie felt his friends pushing him forward.

"Okay, let's go! We can make it this time!" yelled Spunky.

Jamie stepped forward and in an instant he was at the counter.

"Put your money in the jar!" said Steve Yeager.

Automatically, Jamie pulled the coin from his pocket and plinked it into the jar. He had tried to get a good look at the faces of the boys who had just finished shooting. He'd wanted to see if there was any clue to what they felt like when they finished.

But he had only caught a glimpse, and they looked as normal as anybody could look. And suddenly, the rifle was in his hands and he could feel the unexpected weight of the thing.

God, it felt so *real*.

It wasn't like the BB guns he'd shot at galleries before. It was full of detail and mass. And it was comfortable in his hands, as though it had been crafted just for him. His fingers slipped under the front stock and through the trigger guard with a smooth, natural movement. Like he'd been doing it all his life.

"Okay, here we go," said Spunky, who had already taken aim into the darkness.

Following his cue, Jamie raised the rifle and squinted down the barrel, looking into the gallery.

Up until that point, the interior of the wagon was just a blank, a nothingness, which lacked depth, dimension, or light. But as Jamie sighted down the barrel, it was like peering into the center of a collapsed star. For a moment the effect was dizzying, and he wondered if the others felt the same instant of disequilibrium. And then the inside of the wagon seemed to expand and deepen, opening itself up in some kind of relativistic, non-Euclidean space. Jamie was staring into a bottomless, endless enclosure of space. It was like Magister had captured a piece of the darkest, deepest night sky Jamie had ever seen, and stuffed it into the wagon. It was like he could step forward into the farthest reaches of the galaxy.

And then the faces began to appear.

Like ghosts or demons, they materialized out of the night. Floating, weaving. First close and then impossibly far away, the targets moved with an incredible grace and beauty. The faces seemed to glow from some inner light source, each one independent and specially colored and textured. A myriad of shades and colors, always changing, always captivating. Though there was no music, Jamie's mind supplied a balletic score as the targets danced.

And when he squeezed off the first of the rounds, he saw majestic tracers of light, penetrating the darkness, and traveling for an eternity of distance before piercing the targets like laser beams. There was no sound of the rounds being fired, no loud ratcheting or barking of the rifle's chambers. Rather it was an almost silent click of the trigger letting go and the whispering *hiss* of the light beams as they penciled away from the dark barrels. The faces, upon being struck, would flare briefly in a crimson hue, then disappear, only to be replaced by new faces.

And the variety of faces was endless. The images were a blend of many styles and graphic possibilities. Cartoonish and caricatured, photographic and abstract, the faces became bizarre symbols for every emotional human response, every shape and size and type. It was a storm of faces, a torrent.

And he fired at them.

Pulling the trigger was part of the ritual. It was as though he had become an organic part of the movement which choreographed itself in the crazy, unreal distances before him. The music grew louder in his mind and he seemed to be firing with more speed, more accuracy, as though there was a subtle climax building. Aim and fire. Aim and fire. The sequence became an automatic response, as simple and as natural as taking a breath.

The blur of faces began to move at a more frantic pace, and still he kept up with its wildly kinetic seduction. Jamie stared into the strange darkness with a kind of predatory anticipation, almost being able to predict each upcoming movement and trajectory. The sensation was hypnotic and intoxicating. It was like what he'd always imagined it must be like to be flying on some crazy drug. A sense of exhilaration and power came spinning up through the core of his being, whirling and slashing into the forefront of his mind. And along with power came the knowledge. Until he knew what he would be seeing in the next instant.

Until he saw it.

CHAPTER 20

How could she have lost him so easily!?

The crowd had not seemed so overwhelming until Stella tried to pick Jamie's face from its moving panorama. But she knew they were only temporarily separated. Jamie would not have deserted her on purpose.

Stella walked back toward the edge of the crowd, away from the gallery. Maybe he had gone back to where they had parked their ten-speeds.

When she reached the edge of the crowd, past the lemonade stand and the brace of young maple trees, she saw their bicycles leaning against the trees, unattended. Where could he have gone? She felt a renewed burst of anger at Mr. Dutton for interrupting her in the first place. If she hadn't stopped to listen to his nonsense, she would be with Jamie right now.

Looking back at the gathering, she spotted many familiar faces, none of them Jamie's. Without him, she felt so alone. Without knowing it, he had given her the strength and the confidence to pursue her suspicions. Without him by her side, she felt weak and indecisive.

She needed him.

Still standing outside the main body of the crowd, she suddenly saw it as a single entity, a large, featureless, amorphous beast. It was a shape-shifter, an ever-moving, always changing *thing*. For a moment, she was reminded of her dream, and thought the crowd looked very much like the inexorable, amoebalike fog of her nightmare. Even as she stood watching the crowd, it seemed to grow thicker, more impenetrable.

Stella's instincts told her to back away, to avoid the dense anonymity of the crowd, but she knew she had to find Jamie.

Stepping forward, she entered their midst as one might enter an angry surf after dark. Tentative, cautious, she let the odors and sights of the crowd subsume her. Once inside the crowd, she lost all sense of size and proportion. She could have been adrift in a vast sea of faces, a sea which spilled far beyond the modest boundaries of the meadow. Looking in all directions, she could see no end to the crush of bodies.

And she could not see Jamie.

The first twinges of desperation gnawed at the edges of her thoughts. She began to feel a burning need to find him. Something was wrong, and although she could not pinpoint the cause of her sudden fear, she knew it was real, and she knew she would feel better if Jamie were with her.

At first she thought it was only her imagination, but she sensed a surliness in the crowd, a growing sense of something hostile and alien. The crowd seemed to be emanating a collective aura that could only be called evil, or at least dangerous.

Slowly she worked her way through the crowd, nodding and trying to smile at people she recognized. She saw some more kids from school, familiar shopkeepers and their families. She even thought she glimpsed her Aunt Leah, but her mother's sister had not seen her, and had not responded when Stella cried out to her. She saw people she knew, but no one actually acknowledged her. No smiles were returned. Stella was an intruder here, an outsider. What was happening?

Some of them might have been calling her name, and someone reached out, grasping her arm, holding her for an instant before she could break free. She was starting to get scared now. Someone else tried to reach out, touch her, hold her. The crowd seemed to grow thicker and taller. Stella felt as though she were in the center of an impassable thicket—vulnerable and trapped.

She moved through them in a nightmare. Their faces were becoming distorted, exaggerated, like in fun-house mirrors. Their voices had begun to slur together, murmuring in some strange syncopation like an unintelligible chorus of cicada in a million trees, a low-frequency sound, rhythmic and menacing. She had never heard the voices in a crowd seem so much in concert, as though the mob had assumed a single life and purpose of its own.

She cried out for Jamie, but he didn't answer her.

The crowd seemed to be closing in on her, a fist tightening its grip.

Her heart was racing now, her breath ragged and raspy in her throat. She had to find Jamie. *Now*.

Stella moved closer to the gallery, where the

crowd grew even more densely packed, and she could smell the mixture of odors wafting off them. It was a vile stew of nicotine and beer, sweat and perfume, cut grass and damp earth. She felt that she might suffocate if she did not get away. The murmuring grew louder, stronger, as she pushed her way closer to the gallery. The odd cadence of the sound seemed to be calling her name.

The crowd closed in, and she moved still closer to the gallery. She had to get away.

Where was Jamie?

All she wanted to do was find him. They would go away from this place and never come back . . .

The crowd surged forward, turning her around, expelling her into a small open space before the gallery.

She saw him.

Jamie. Right in front of her.

His narrow frame leaned against the counter, the rifle nestled against his cheek, his face partially hidden by his long brown hair.

Betrayal swept through Stella like a molten liquid. It burned a path into the deepest core of her being and there turned heavy and cold. How could he do this to her? She felt angry, but did not know why. On the surface Jamie had done nothing terrible. But his actions disturbed and distressed her. What had happened? She didn't understand anything anymore. Everything was getting crazy. It wasn't supposed to be like this. Her thoughts thrashed about in a tangled mass of confusion and hurt. Her pain was almost a palpable thing as she stared at him with still, disbelieving eyes.

"Jamie!" She cried out his name without regard to those around her. It was a heartfelt, plaintive cry which conveyed her pain to anyone who might hear it.

But no one did. Not even Jamie.

The people buzzed around her, oblivious to her cry above the general din; Jamie continued to fire into the darkness of the wagon.

Without thinking, she left the edge of the crowd and reached out to him. As her hand touched his shoulder, she could feel him tense up. Startled, he turned and looked at her with a shock in his eyes, as though she'd jolted him with high voltage.

"Jamie?"

He stared at her, eyes wide, as though seeing something far away. There was a conflux of emotions in his face—surprise, wonder, confusion, and even anger.

"What?" he shouted. "What the hell are you doing?"

Stella was taken back by his outburst, by the vacant and disoriented look in his eyes.

"Jamie, what's the matter with you!?"

The sound of her voice seemed to reach him this time. She watched as his eyes began to focus upon her and the shock and anger drained from his face.

There was a terrible pain building in her chest, ready to explode, and she couldn't keep it in any longer.

"Jamie, how could you?" she screamed, still not certain why she was so upset.

"Stella, wait, I can explain!"

He started to speak, but she pulled away from him. Everyone now seemed aware of her fear and pain and disappointment, and she had no wish to share it with any of them. This was not the place to confront Jamie, and at that moment, the way she was hurting inside, she just wanted to be away from him.

She was running through the crowd now, pushing people out of the way. Jamie's voice, calling out her name, seemed impossibly far behind her.

Turning toward the trees by the shoulder of the road, she was suddenly aware of a shape looming in the shadows beyond the light and color of the clearing. Stella moved forward as the shape took form and substance. It was the carnival man, Mister Magister, who stood silent and watchful. His black cape swept about him like a shroud, making him tall and thin. There was a gaunt and ghostly quality to his face which made her want to look away.

But she could not.

Against her will, she stared into the depths of Magister's eyes—dark, obsidian pits from which heat and light could never escape. He stood so still that he could have been a figure from a wax museum, but she could feel his attention focused upon her like a tight beam of light. It was a chilling sensation which hunched her shoulders, and the movement helped her break eye contact with the man.

How can they all come out here and look at him and not be afraid? To Stella, it seemed obvious, but was she the only one to really see him?

She unchained her bike and moved off in a daze. The road back into town stretched ahead of her like the slick, molted skin of a black snake. Without lights or reflectors, and not caring about either, she leaned into the wind and pedaled as fast as she could.

How could Jamie *do* it? She and Jamie were supposed to be different, weren't they?

The thought kept repeating, each time bringing a new round of pain.

As she neared the outskirts of the town, she looked up at the night sky, speckled with starlight, and felt terribly alone and adrift. A feeling of insignificance, of worthlessness, fell over her like a shroud, and warm tears stained her wind-chapped cheeks. She felt silly for crying, but there was nothing left to do, other than run off into the night and hide.

She hated Jamie and Aunt Leah and all of them.

She loved them, too.

It was just so hard to feel so much pain, and not be able to do anything about it.

Finally she reached her home. Stella put the bike in the garage and went straight up to her room. The image of Jamie hunkered over the counter, firing into the gallery, would not leave her. It seemed burned into her mind like an overexposed negative. Teary and upset, she undressed by moonlight and stood by the window, thinking about how empty the town was at that moment, and how no one seemed to care.

Climbing into bed, she could not calm her thoughts. Even though her body ached and cried for sleep, she knew it would not come. Stella reached for her journal and a pen, knowing that the only therapy would be to write down her tangled thoughts, to make some order from the chaos of her emotions and pain.

Perhaps if she could get it down on paper, even badly, even awkwardly, things would not seem so bad.

But she knew that they were.

CHAPTER 21

Magister watched.

The people of this town had embraced him and his device with a passion. He smiled knowingly. It was not a welcome unaccustomed to him. The colored lights, the partylike atmosphere, the heavy aromas of cheap foods and dense crowds were all too familiar to him. Always different, but in some essential, universal ways, always the same.

Sometimes he wearied of his task. Tonight had been just such a night . . . until the return of the special one. He had been thinking that most sentient beings make such a celebration of their rise to that state called civilization. He had been thinking that most of that state was a sham, a disguise, a thinly constructed illusion.

There was an arrogance and a rigid structure about these beings which bothered him. The outer shell of their culture exhibited a pride, a strength, and a massiveness not unlike one of their Gothic cathedrals; but also like those great stone buildings, their society, on the inside, appeared vast, empty, and full of curious echoes.

They tried to be so proper and correct, but the landscapes of their minds rattled with the chained phantoms of every fear and prejudice ever known. There was a primal chaos still within them. Like the molten core of a planet, still sending columns of magma to the encrusted surface, so did these beings still erupt with the stuff of their most primordial selves.

He knew they were preparing the way for their own inevitable destruction, and he knew that he would be the instrument. They would bring it upon themselves and then blame him, never knowing that he was just a tool in their own twisted hands. Magister had seen it all before. A thousand times, a thousand civilizations, a thousand different ways he had been the bringer of biological entropy, the love-death of a species which did not quite scale the heights of true intelligence and compassion.

Magister smiled as he recalled the passing of some he had truly loathed, and others he had regretted.

He watched the humans until the night burned itself out. Sated and exhausted, they moved off to their shelters at last, and Magister wiped their stench from the weapons, closed up the fold-down counter. A deceptive silence swept across the meadow like a dark wind. He could still hear the primitive roaring of their souls, an echo which refused to fade away completely.

But he had detected another sound that night. Soft and tentative. Full of fear and suspicion, but still a sincere, earnest sound. It was the flutter of delicate wings. The wings of a solitary creature attempting to fly above the coming chaos.

CHAPTER 22

"Stella?" called Aunt Leah. Her voice strained to carry up the stairs and down the hall. "Stella, Jamie's here to see you!"

Stella lay on her bed, staring up at the ceiling. She didn't want to see him; she didn't even want to answer her aunt.

Jamie.

She had avoided him all day at school, even when he came up to her in the cafeteria. She could not look at him without seeing him leaning across the counter, shooting into the darkness. But not talking to him made her feel cut off, adrift from everything. She had had a feeling that he would come to the house after school, and part of her was happy that he had, but she could not see him.

Not now. Not while the hurt was still so new.

"Stella, did you hear me? Jamie's here!"

Getting up, she dragged herself to the door, called down the stairs.

"I heard you," she said. "Tell him I can't see him right now. Please, Auntie . . ."

"What?" Aunt Leah sounded shocked. Stella

heard her footsteps on the stairs. In a moment she was standing on the threshold to Stella's bedroom, staring at her niece. "What seems to be the trouble, Stella?"

"Nothing."

"Nothing? That boy's standing on the front porch with a face as long as a mule's, and you're up here moping like you're sick, and you're going to tell me there's nothing wrong?" Aunt Leah chuckled and walked close to Stella, reached out to take her hand. "Did you two have your first fight? Want to tell me about it?"

Stella shook her head slowly. Her aunt would not understand. The woman was assuming there was a problem in puppy-love-land, when it was so much more than that. Stella could never even begin to explain what she was feeling, what she had seen, and worse, what she thought was going on in the town.

"Stella, Jamie is waiting for you downstairs. If you won't talk to me, then go talk to him."

Her aunt was right. Stella had a burning need to talk to someone, and the only person in the world who could listen, who could understand what she was feeling, was Jamie.

"All right," she said, sighing a bit dramatically. "Could you please tell him I'll be down in a minute?"

Aunt Leah nodded, allowing a small smile to form at the corners of her mouth. She turned and exited the room. Stella checked her face and hair in the mirror. Her eyes were not too red. She looked presentable.

Downstairs, Jamie was sitting on the porch swing. His lean face indeed looked long and hangdog. He looked at her with sad, shiny, spaniel eyes.

"I had to stop by and try to talk to you," he said.

"I'm glad you did."

"You are?" His expression changed a few degrees, edging toward relief.

"Jamie, it's just that . . . Well, *why*?"

"I've been trying to tell you all day, but you wouldn't let me."

She looked at him and almost smiled. He was certainly right about that. "I'm sorry, but I was feeling bad. I felt like you turned on me, like you deserted me. Do you know what I mean?"

"Sure I do. But all of a sudden you were gone. I couldn't find you."

"I got caught by Mr. Dutton." She shuddered. "What a creep he is!"

"I felt terrible when I heard you, and when I saw you looking at me. It was awful, Stella."

"I know."

"Listen, we've got to talk. I've got some stuff to tell you."

She could tell that he was intensely serious. Something that might be terror seemed to be hiding behind his eyes.

Stella nodded. She went inside for a moment, telling her aunt she was going for a walk, then returned to the porch. Neither of the teenagers spoke again until they were on the sidewalk, heading up Madison toward Sycamore. They turned left at the corner and headed west toward Grover's Road and the old mill.

"Stella, listen, I'm sorry if I hurt you when I went to the gallery, but I couldn't find you." Jamie explained to her how he'd met the guys from school, and how he just kind of fell into step with them. "Besides, I figured it was important that we know what's going on with that wagon, why everybody's so gonzo about it.''

"Did you find out?''

"Stella, you wouldn't believe it! You've got to try it yourself.''

She felt herself tense at the words. "No! No, I couldn't do it. I *know* I couldn't. There's something wrong with that shooting gallery. It's not just Magister we should be worrying about.''

Jamie looked at her with a touch of awe and respect in his gaze. "Jeez, what makes you think that, Stella?''

"I'm not sure, it's just something I feel.''

"Well, listen. I have to tell you what it was like.''

"You sound excited," she said. "Did you . . . did you like it? Like everybody else does?''

"It's hard to explain like that. It's more like you don't even think about liking it or not liking it while you're up there, Stella. You just *do* it.''

"It sounds like a drug, Jamie. It sounds awful.''

"No, it's not like it has control over you. You can do what you want, and you can stop whenever you want." Jamie cleared his throat, paused as they continued walking. "It's hard to explain, I guess.''

"You're not being very clear," said Stella. She wanted to be patient and give him a chance. She had to be careful not to sound too nasty to him.

"I know, I know. It's like a video game, I guess. You get so wrapped up in it that you kind of go on automatic pilot. And that's easy to do because the whole display is so amazing.''

"What do you mean?''

Jamie spent a few minutes explaining how the interior of the gallery produced an illusion of size and depth much greater than the actual physical dimensions of the wagon. He told her how exhilarating it was to stare into the darkness, and how captivating the overall effect was. She understood what he meant, and the knowledge just scared her more. It only underscored her convictions that there was something weird going on with the gallery.

But there had to be more to it than just that. She had the feeling that Jamie knew more than he was saying.

"Is that everything?" asked Stella. "That's what you wanted to tell me so badly?"

"Well, yeah, I guess." Jamie's expression changed from one of sincere concern to one of guilt. He looked at her with difficulty, and she thought she could detect a rising fear behind his eyes. Jamie was holding back because it scared him—she was sure of it.

"Jamie," she asked slowly, "there's something else, isn't there?"

"No . . . yes." He looked away, up at the sky, then back at her. There was real terror in his eyes now. "Oh, Jeez, Stella, it's crazy! It's awful!"

She stopped and touched his shoulder. They were standing at the intersection to Grover's Road, and she felt very open and exposed. She'd never seen him like this and it was unsettling. It was making her paranoid. "Jamie, what is it?"

"I've been wanting to tell you, but it's hard, Stella." He looked around, as though people in the nearby houses might be listening.

"You can tell me now," she said, seeing that he shared her sudden awareness that no one should hear what they were talking about. The neighborhood was quiet and serene. "There's nobody around."

Jamie nodded, drew a deep breath, and attempted to compose himself. She was dying to know what he was going to tell her, but she felt she shouldn't push him. He would tell her; the time had to be right, that's all.

"It *is* Magister, isn't it?" she said. "I was right all along, wasn't I?"

"I think so. He's part of it, that's for sure."

Stella nodded as they reached the end of the block. Across the street, flanking Nelson's Little League field, were stands for the summer crowds of parents and girlfriends. But the bleachers were deserted now, and Jamie led her to the lower benches.

"All right," he said, sighing. "Listen . . ."

Stella moved next to him on the bench and took his hand in hers. She closed her eyes and concentrated on what he was saying.

"I told you about the targets being faces," he began. "Well, they're always changing, always moving. You don't really get to study any of them very much because there isn't any time. Plus you're always shooting them and they're blinking out and new ones are coming up. You with me so far?"

"Yes," she said, squeezing his hand.

"Okay. So last night, I'm shooting and just for a second or two, I saw a different face." He paused and drew a long breath, exhaled slowly.

"Different? Different how?"

Jamie looked at her, his eyes steady, his hand trembling slightly. "It was different because it was *real*, Stella."

Her mind refused to process and accept the words. "What do you mean?"

"I mean it was somebody I know. Somebody we all know. I saw his face in the gallery, Stella."

"Oh, God, Jamie! Who was it? Who did you see?"

"Mr. Liebowitz."

She felt her stomach knotting up, threatening to drop away like a lead weight. In an instant, it all made sense to her. There was no denying what was going on, but *how*? And *why*? And how could Jamie be a part of this thing? This crazy, perverted mess.

"And you . . . you just kept shooting anyway?"

"Stella, wait, you don't understand! It was just for a second or two! You didn't have time to think about it, not really."

"Oh, Jamie, don't you see what's happening?"

"Of course I do! That's why I'm so scared, Stella. I feel sick inside. Way down deep, I feel sick."

She nodded, now intimately familiar with the terror which seemed to slither and slip within her.

"Now I *know* we have to do something. We can't just sit around and wait for Magister to kill Mr. Liebowitz."

"How are we going to stop him?" Jamie sounded incredulous.

"I don't know, but we've got to try," she said. "We've got to warn people in town. We've got to tell them what's happening here."

"Stella, wait a minute. We really don't have anything to tell anybody, don't you see? That's what I've been worried about ever since I put it together myself. Ever since I saw old Mr. Liebowitz's face in there . . ."

She didn't answer him right away. Even without thinking over everything they knew about Magister, she knew that it was all supposition and what Jamie would call gut reaction. Without any concrete proof, it would be almost impossible to get anyone to listen. And why would Magister want to kill people in her town? There was no motive, no reason. How was he doing it? It was all so irrational, so bizarre. It was like a nightmare in which things *almost* hung together, almost made sense, but not quite.

Jamie was looking at her, as though waiting for a magical solution.

"Jamie, you're right, I know, but I still feel we have to do something." She paused, and the only possible solution came to her. "There is *one* thing we could do."

"What?"

"Go see Mr. Liebowitz."

"What, and tell him that a carnival man is trying to kill him?" Jamie shook his head. "No way!"

He was right again. Just because a teenager thinks he saw a shooting gallery funny face that looked like the town's shoemaker didn't mean that the man was going to die. At least that's how Mr. Liebowitz would think, and when you looked at it like that, Stella couldn't very well blame him. It did sound ridiculous.

"Well, let's just walk by his shop, at least," she said.

"Jeez, Stella, what for?"

"I don't know. I guess I'll just feel better. If we see him in there working, maybe I won't feel so scared. Do you know what I mean?"

"Sure I do." He smiled thinly, then nodded. "Okay, come on. It's not far."

Cutting up Jefferson and taking a right on Center Street, they headed toward the middle of town. As the hour crept toward five o'clock, the traffic grew a bit heavier, although it never got very jammed up.

There were lots of people on the sidewalks in front of all the shops, and it looked like a perfectly normal Indian summer afternoon.

Stella hoped sincerely that it was.

The narrow, little windows of the shoe repair shop looked dark and empty as Jamie stopped in front to peer through the dusty glass.

"It looks like he's closed," he said, his voice fading away.

"Jamie, I don't like this. He's never shut down during the week."

"Maybe it's some kind of Jewish holiday," he said. "Don't they have something around this time of year?"

"I don't know," said Stella. "Let's ask around, see if anyone knows anything."

Jamie nodded and headed toward the door of the adjacent record shop, the Turntable. Stella followed him inside, where a handful of young people idled over the bins of albums. Stella identified the dark-haired, gum-chewing girl behind the register as a senior at school, but if she recognized Stella, she did not acknowledge it.

"Excuse me," said Jamie as he approached the cashier. "Do you know why the shoemaker's closed next door?"

The girl cracked her gum and shrugged. "How should I know? I just came in about an hour ago."

It seemed to Stella that the cashier's attitude typified the level of concern about what was going on in Brampton. No big deal. Not my problem. Not my job. It was getting predictable, but no less scary.

Jamie did not back down. "Well, what about the manager? Is he here? Would he know?"

The girl tilted her head and raised her eyebrows. "I guess. He's in the back room. Just knock on the door with the mirror on it."

Jamie took Stella's hand and walked with her to the back of the store.

Following Jamie's knock, the manager appeared. He was a nice-looking man in his early thirties.

"What can I do for you kids?"

"I wanted to pick up my boots from next door, but it's all closed up," said Jamie. "I was just wondering if you could tell me why?"

The manager shook his head, grinned ever so slightly. "You mean Liebowitz? Man, they carried him outa there this morning. Must've died in his sleep or something."

The word stung, but the sickening wave which followed was a dull aftershock. Stella had anticipated the news, had almost known that the old man would be dead. It was part of the whole process, wasn't it? The bigger question was how and why this Magister character was doing it. Stella wanted to cry but could not. Crying would be a release, but she was too bound up by unanswerable questions. There was no chance of a simple emotional discharge.

Though she had never really known the old shoemaker, a wave of nausea passed over her as she conjured the image of the medic carrying out his lonely, still form. Liebowitz had lived alone and had died alone. There was an essential human sadness in dying alone, and she grieved for him.

"Oh, jeez, I didn't know . . ." she heard Jamie saying. The sound of his voice seemed very far away even though he was standing right next to her.

Taking her hand, Jamie guided her from the store.

"Come on, Stella." His voice was flat, and she knew that he was stunned and shocked, and as terrified as she.

"Jamie, what are we going to do?"

"I don't know. I feel *awful,* Stella. What can we do?"

They walked toward Jefferson Avenue. Townspeople passed them with a hurried indifference. Stella noted the blandness of their faces, and she wondered what was happening to everybody. Did they always look like this? So faceless, as cold and hard as cut stone . . .

"I feel like we should go talk to somebody. Chief Nelson or maybe Father Doheny. Somebody like that," she said, but there was no energy in her voice. Even she did not believe it would do any good.

"The good old authority figures," said Jamie. "Somehow I think that would be a bust . . ."

Stella shivered. Someone had walked over her grave—that's what Aunt Leah would have said. She shook her head at the thought. Someone was walking over *all* of their graves, but no one seemed to care.

"Where are we going now?" asked Jamie. He sounded lost and helplessly adrift.

She stopped and looked at him as they reached the street corner. "Jamie, I'm scared. I want to be with you for a while."

He nodded. "You want to go to the mill?"

"Yes," she said.

Without another word, they turned down Jefferson and headed for Grover's Road. Despite the terror which was lurking at the edges of Stella's conscious mind, the terror which she was fighting to keep in the outer dark, she felt a spark of excitement gathering heat within her breast.

Jamie. Alone with Jamie.

The idea warmed her, gave her strength.

Out of nowhere, thoughts of the book in her sweater drawer, *The Facts of Life and Love,* came to her. In the midst of the fear and the uncertainty, she found herself wanting him. It was crazy, but there was a delicious thrill in just having the thought. If there existed a power to banish the cold darkness of abject fear, perhaps this was it.

"It's not that far," Jamie said as they passed through the final block of houses at the edge of town, and the rolling fields of Iowa broke free once again.

Stella nodded. They cut across Nelson's Field and cleared a copse of trees. The ruined cedar shake of the old mill huddled in the overgrowth like a forgotten tombstone. Stella could feel the solitude of the place. There was a sense of age, of history about it. Ghosts of past generations of mill workers still gathered here.

Guiding her through the brambles and stickerbushes to a small door, Jamie spoke softly: "This way in. Be careful where you put your feet."

Stella followed him into the falling-down building. There were holes in the flooring, and sunlight shafted through big gashes in the roof. The center of the main room still held the big wooden gears and millstones which had once been kept churning by the power of the stream. It was an old, rotting place, but it did not have an atmosphere of forboding about it. Rather, Stella felt a certain comfort in knowing that they were truly alone there, safe from the prying of others in the town.

Jamie walked ahead, passing through the main part of the building into a brace of smaller rooms that must have served as offices. One was furnished with shelves, old chairs, and a davenport, violated by time and the occasional vandal. Jamie moved to the old sofa which was flowered with exploded blossoms of stuffing. He sat down and gestured that she join him.

Looking into his eyes, she wondered if his thoughts were similar to her own. She sat close to him and put her head on his shoulder. Jamie put his arm around her. There was an awkwardness in his movements. Stella sensed his lack of confidence and found it charming. Despite the tension and stress, it was nice to feel herself starting to smile.

"Well," said Jamie. "Here we are . . ." His hand patted her shoulder, lightly touched the flesh of her upper arm.

Stella gazed into his eyes, then down at the configuration of the slatted wood floor. "What's going to happen to us, Jamie? Do you ever think about that?"

"Lately, yes. But I keep thinking we're too young to have to worry about stuff like that."

"I know what you mean, but we don't have much choice. I'm scared, Jamie. If I keep thinking about what's happening all the time, I don't know what'll happen to me." Stella wasn't sure what she was feeling at that moment, or what she might say next. The words just poured out. "I need to get my mind off of everything, even if it's for just a little while."

"Okay," Jamie said, then fell silent. His arm lay inert across her shoulders, his hand still patting her arm inanely.

She could feel his nervousness. Either he didn't know what to do or he didn't know what she wanted. Or both. There was only one way to get things moving.

"Jamie, would you kiss me?"

"What? Oh, *sure* . . ."

He looked straight into her eyes as his face drew close to hers. She blinked as his long lashes brushed her own, then closed her eyes. As if by magic, their lips found each other's. The contact was soft at first, barely touching, then he pressed forward, and Stella had the urge to open her mouth, to do it the way they did it in the movies. She felt a tingling sensation flood down from her breasts, all through her body.

After an immeasurable time, Jamie drew back and opened his eyes. They were dark and wet and deep. Beautiful eyes. "That was nice," he said. "Do it again?"

She giggled. "Why not?"

And that was how it started. The first tentative contact grew into a more practiced, more confident act of joy. Stella had the feeling that she could be swept away, carried off in a state of mind she'd never known possible. Jamie was holding her now, and it was with a strength and knowledge she had longed for.

His hands had slipped beneath her sweater at the small of her back, where her shirt tail had slipped free of her jeans. The feel of his hands upon her soft flesh was incredible, unreal. She wanted him to move his hands all over her.

There was an innocence in what they did, but it was laced with desire. Sexual desire, certainly, but also the need to know the unknown, to pull back the veil and finally see what had been kept from them. It would be so wonderful, so beautiful, she thought. She knew it would be.

Jamie tried to speak her name, but his voice was less than a whisper. He was trembling. She could feel his own desire building, a sweet, innocent yearning. It was, for that moment, the only real thing in the whole world.

She leaned back and slowly reclined upon the old davenport. Still clinging to her, Jamie descended with her, and after a moment's odd shifting of weight and position, they lay side by side. She could smell the musty age of the couch's upholstery which mixed and clashed with the herbal scent of his freshly shampooed hair. His hands moved beneath her sweater, so slowly, a warm glacial movement as they slipped along the sides of her waist. She waited and waited for the touch which never seemed to come.

Jamie wanted her.

And she wanted him.

Stella refused to let herself think about the rightness or wrongness of what they were doing. It did not matter. She had pushed into the harsh reality of the world of hate and deception and death, and if she had to face these realities, then it was only fair that she also partake of some of the world's more pleasurable aspects.

Jamie had moved his hand to her stomach now. As they kissed, she opened her mouth slightly, and let her tongue explore the inner edges of her lips, flirting with his. The contact set off an electric charge between them. She could feel it down to her toes and she knew Jamie as well had been tapped into its magic amperage.

Spurred on by this new pleasure, Jamie responded and she felt the tips of his fingers ever so lightly brushing the softness of her skin just below her bra. Up moved his fingers and just for an instant she felt his touch upon the softness of her young breasts.

He touched her again. His fingers brushed across her nipple, making it tingle with sensation, making it flush and harden almost instantly. She had never imagined it would be like this.

She arched her back, pressing herself closer to him, closer to his touch. She was pleased with his gentleness. In her heart of hearts, Stella had known that he would be, but it was gratifying to know that she had been right.

He pulled away, looking into her eyes. "Stella, what are we doing here?" he asked in a whisper. "Is this okay?"

"I don't know. I don't know if anything is ever okay, do you?" She grinned impishly.

"Huh?" Jamie could not hide his confusion.

Stella knew that he only wanted to know if they should go on or stop. She found it interesting that he would defer to her, as though she were more capable of making that decision. But maybe that's the way it was with boys. They were so maddeningly driven to sex that they looked to girls to provide them with a measure of control over it.

He looked at her, waiting.

"Jamie, I don't know . . . I really don't know."

He swallowed and nodded. "Stella, you're really beautiful, and so special to me—I guess I'm trying to tell you that this is kind of scary, do you understand?"

She nodded. "Of course it is. It seems like everything in our lives is getting scary all at once, doesn't it?"

"Maybe we should stop . . ." Jamie's hands were around her waist. There was a warmth and a strength in his embrace.

"Maybe—"

"Not because I *want* to stop. Jeez, I could stay like this *forever* . . . but I keep thinking that maybe we're not ready for this yet. I just don't know."

Although her body still danced with crazy sensations, she knew that he was being sensible. He was asking for her help to stop, so that they would have more time to prepare for what lay ahead for them.

"No," she said, after a pause. "You're right, Jamie. And it's getting late, anyway. My aunt's going to wonder where I am. She gets worried so easy."

He looked at his watch, nodded. "Yeah, it's almost five-thirty."

Helping Stella up from the couch, Jamie had trouble looking her in the eye. Since she had felt more in control of the situation, she did not feel so awkward. He was so bright and confident most of the time that it was fascinating to see him in this new light.

Without speaking, they straightened their clothes and left the old mill. The afternoon sun was just visible above the trees, and the air was losing its warmth. Stella didn't care how cold it might get—a flame had been ignited in her heart and it burned with the true heat of love and desire. She knew that no matter what else might happen, she would never lose the comfort of that warmth.

They walked back across the baseball field and down Sycamore Street, mostly in silence. But it was not an awkward silence, it was a shared communion. They did not need to speak, and Stella liked that.

Before they parted on her front porch, she stole a quick kiss and slipped inside the house. Jamie would call after dinner.

It was time to reenter the real world.

CHAPTER 23

It was the fourth day of madness.

The thought came to Tilden Strong as he stood behind the cash register, counting out the day's receipts. It made him lose track of where he was, forcing him to clear his pocket calculator and begin again. As the numbers marched through his mind, he could not keep the alien thought from intruding. At this rate, he would never close the store; he would never get home.

Maybe that wouldn't be so bad . . .

Then he wouldn't have to eat a hastily prepared dinner before escorting Louisa and Joanna out to the meadow. He had been telling himself that they were the only reason he had been going back ever since that first night. If it wasn't for them, he wouldn't be there.

The little bell at the front door jangled, and he glanced down at his watch, then up toward the entrance. Watching Stella Chambers walk to the cold-cabinet, he thought about how quickly she was growing up, and how pretty a young lady she had become. Long strawberry-blond hair, big green eyes, and the most engaging smile. Yes, she looked like somebody's homecoming queen, all right.

"You're almost too late, Stella," he said, trying to force a smile to his face. "It's five of six . . ."

"I'm sorry, Mr. Strong. My aunt ran out of butter right before dinner and she sent me up for some." She looked at the open cash drawer and the torn-off register tape next to the calculator. "Did you already close out the register?"

"It's okay, I'll just ring you up on tomorrow's tape."

"Oh, good. Thanks."

He punched in the keys, announced the total, and Stella handed him the exact amount. "How is Leah these days?" he asked as he bagged the pound box of butter. "I saw her down to the meadow the other night . . ."

Stella's features darkened at that instant. "I know," she said, her eyes cast down as though embarrassed or saddened. "She goes there every night with her friends. Just like everybody else."

Tilden was tempted to let the remark pass. It would have been easy to ignore, but there was a gnawing in his gut, a sinking feeling in his conscience, which made him speak.

"I know, Stella. It's . . . it's bad, isn't it?" The words felt dry in his mouth. He felt his hands beginning to tremble as he pushed the bag across the counter.

She looked up at him, surprised. And something ignited behind her eyes which looked suspiciously like hope.

"Mr. Strong, you're the first person I've talked to who's said anything like that. Since that shooting gallery came here, it's been crazy!"

Her candor shocked Tilden into silence. He hadn't actually wanted to talk about it. He had only wanted her to know that he understood. But what good was that? He suspected that deep down, *everyone* understood.

"Mr. Strong?" She was looking at him.

"Yes, Stella?"

"You *do* know what I mean, don't you?"

"Well . . ." Better to drop the whole thing. He wanted to get counted out and get home.

Stella ignored the butter as she stared at him. Her eyes were as green as the sea, her gaze as sharp as a lance.

"Mr. Strong, you're afraid. I know. So am I. Oh, God, I've been wondering if anybody else noticed, if anybody cared."

"Stella, I know what you're going to say, but it's crazy to think that—"

"To think what? That three people have died in Brampton in *three days?* Ever since that carnival man, that Mister Magister, came to town!"

Strong looked away, toward the door, hoping that some last-minute shopper might barge in and interrupt this conversation. Stella was invading his secret thoughts, making him face the fears that had been leering and capering on the edge of his day-to-day thoughts, the fears that he had been almost successfully avoiding.

"Coincidence," he said weakly. "It's just a coincidence . . ."

"You don't believe that," said Stella, "any more than I do."

"Stella—"

"Something weird is happening here, Mr. Strong. It's like there's been a cloak thrown over the whole town. Something awful is happening to us, and everybody's trying to make believe that nothing is wrong!"

Tilden knew that what she was saying was dead on the money. He nodded in spite of his desire to remain uninvolved.

"You've been down to the gallery, haven't you, Mr. Strong?"

"Yes, I have."

She appeared saddened by his answer. "I never thought you were the type for guns or games, Mr. Strong."

He shrugged. "You never can tell, I guess."

"Tell me about the faces."

"You mean the targets? Why, there's nothing to tell, really. They're just funny faces, that's all. You shoot at them. That's it."

"Is it *really*?"

What was she trying to do to him? She knew damned well what was going on. Why was she trying to get him to admit something he had told himself he would never talk about?

"Tell me what happens!" Stella insisted.

Stella stood facing him, her hands on her hips in what looked like a defiant posture, but he could see there was pleading in her eyes. He could feel her urgent need to hear her own suspicions or fears confirmed.

"Mr. Strong . . .?"

"You shoot the targets, and they glow and then they just disappear."

"There's more, isn't there?"

He swallowed hard, and nodded.

"Tell me the rest."

He cleared his throat, looked up toward the front door, and then back at the girl. "Other faces take their place and you shoot them, too . . ."

"What other faces?" Stella did not wait for him. Her words poured forth in a steady, rapid-fire stream. They pierced him like a fusillade of bullets. "You see other faces, all right! You saw the faces of the people who died, didn't you?"

He moved back a step from the register, reeling. He nodded quickly, and half-whispered through clenched teeth, "Yes . . . yes, damn it! Oh, Jesus, yes, that's exactly what I saw!"

Stella did not reply immediately. Shock crossed darkly over her features. She had been expecting his answer, but hearing it still repulsed her.

"Jamie was right," she said, "I knew he was. Oh, God, Mr. Strong, we've got to *do* something!"

"What're you talking about? What can we do?"

"I don't know, but we can't go on acting like everybody else! You're a good man, Mr. Strong, you've got to help me!"

He looked at her with a mixture of fear and anger. She was reaching inside, trying to touch that final region, that isolated piece of his soul which had not yet turned into ice. He had been doing so well and now she had come along and ruined everything.

"There's nothing I can do, Stella. There's nothing any of us can do."

"I'll never believe that."

"Listen, Stella. You've got no proof. You can't go barging into this thing half-cocked. That's not the way the world is run."

She smiled satirically. "Oh, and I guess you and the rest of the town run it just fine, right?"

"That's not what I mean, Stella. It's just that it's a complicated world, and you're not old enough to understand everything about it."

"I don't think any of us ever are." There was a burning in her. He remembered his own days of righteous indignation, and the crusading spirit which gave meaning to his life. Perhaps that was what he needed right now—but he was too old, and too tired to pick up any new banners.

"Stella, you're getting yourself too worked up. This thing will pass. He'll go away."

"*When*? How can you be sure? How can you be like this?"

She looked at him with a gut-churning disgust, as though he were a victim of some wasting, leprous disease.

"I don't know what to do!" he cried out, more loudly than he wanted. She had untapped all the fear and horror that he had been keeping under pressure, and now it came bubbling up in a thick hot column, choking him, flooding him with its acid-burning soul-ache. His eyes began to water copiously. Not tears, but a stinging solution of fear and self-loathing.

Stella looked away from him. He must have looked pathetic to her.

"I think I'd better go, Mr. Strong." She turned and headed toward the door without looking back. In that moment he felt overwhelmed by a wildly irrational fear of being left alone in the store.

"Wait!"

The girl paused to look back at him.

For a moment he stood looking at her, slack-jawed and paralytic. He wanted to say that he would help.

He wanted to ask her to stay with him and help him fight against the advancing shadows of evening and the coming dark night of his soul. He tried to reach down to the core of his being, but there was only an emptiness, a dry, hollow, desiccated deadness. None of the words or feelings would come, and he looked dumbly at her.

"Yes, Mr. Strong?"

"I . . . I just wanted to tell you—be careful walking home, okay?"

Stella grimaced sadly. "I think it's time we all were careful, don't you?"

"Well . . ."

"Good-bye, Mr. Strong." Turning quickly, Stella opened the door and was gone.

Time swirled around him like the eddying pool of a foul stream. He stood motionless, thoughtless, as though waiting for the final frostbitten moment when the coming ice would completely envelop him.

Breaking the spell, he turned and picked up the phone, dialing his home. Joanna answered, and he said he was having trouble getting the register tape to come out even, and that he would be a little late. She sounded disappointed, and hinted that she and daughter-dear might not hold supper for him, that they might gobble-gobble as quickly as they could so that they could make the nightly pilgrimage to Harker's meadow.

He nodded and assured her that it would be all right, that he would meet them up there. The walk would do him good, he said.

Hanging up the phone, he looked down at the uncounted money, the unbalanced receipts ledger. He bagged the money in a bank-deposit sack, and stuffed the ledger back under the counter. He could not think of figures now. The books could wait till morning.

Best that he just get out of there. Take that walk and see if he could collect his thoughts.

Get himself together.

He wished that girl had never come in tonight. And yet, maybe it was time everything came to a head . . . ?

He walked out the front door, not bothering to check the lock. He always did, and it was always locked, and tonight would be no different.

But tonight *was* different. He did not know why, but he could feel it.

As he walked east down Center Street, toward the meadow, he was surprised at how quiet and deserted everything seemed, hardly anyone on the sidewalks. When he saw the neon sign for Donnegan's Taproom, it occurred to him that he might enjoy a drink. Or two.

Tilden was not normally a drinking man other than a cold beer after mowing a summer lawn, or a few nutmegged eggnogs at Christmas when Joanna's relatives stopped by. But tonight he had the urge to pour a few shots of fire down his throat. He wanted to feel the shock of the acid-burn in his gullet, and the dull explosion in the base of his gut. He wanted to punish himself a little and then forget.

Pushing through the door, he sought out a stool along the bar, which was only half full of men stopping off for a refresher before heading home.

Tom Donnegan looked at Tilden like he didn't recognize him, and waited for his order.

"George Dickel and a Coke chaser," said Tilden.

The shot glass accompanied by the tumbler of Coke was brought wordlessly and clinked down in front of him. Tilden pulled a five-dollar bill out of his pocket and stretched it out in front of the glasses. He sipped from the Dickel, letting the velvet fire burn and scour the soft tissues of his mouth and throat, resisting the urge to soften the attack with a big gulp of Coke.

A hand slapped his shoulder, and people moved onto the stools on both sides of him.

"Well, well, if it ain't our groceryman," said Joseph Dutton. "Look who's here, Sam."

Dutton chuckled as Tilden nodded at him then looked to his left to see dim-witted Sam Havens gawking and grinning at him.

"Don't see your ass in here very often," said Havens. "Matter of fact, don't think I ever seen you in here."

"There's a first time for everything," said Tilden. *Something awful is happening to us.*

The newcomers ordered drafts of beer which they seemed to inhale almost immediately, and then reordered. Tilden finished his shot, called for another. The two men chattered aimlessly for a bit, including Tilden in the conversation, but not seeming to care that he said little or nothing to keep it going. He didn't really like either of them, but they kept his mind off his own horrors.

Until the talk drifted inevitably, as he knew it would, to the shooting gallery.

"You going down tonight, Mr. Strong?" asked Havens, grinning his silly, almost ever-present grin. His long greasy hair stuck out from beneath his Texaco hat in all directions.

"I don't know, Sam. Maybe not . . ."

I never thought you were the type for guns or games, Mr. Strong.

Havens nodded. "I'll tell you one thing. I'm getting *good* at that thing! I'll outshoot anybody that wants to put a few dollars down, that's for god-damned sure."

I think it's time we all were careful, don't you?

"Better not let Zack Reynolds hear you talkin' like that," said Dutton.

"Shit! Zack couldn't clean my rifle!"

It's like there's been a cloak thrown over the whole town.

"Well," said Tilden, surprising himself, trying to shift the talk to something else, "it won't matter much longer anyway."

Dutton looked at him oddly. "What're you talkin' about?"

Tilden studied his shot glass intently. "Weather gets much colder and that Magister fellow's going to be heading south anyway."

"Oh, yeah, I guess he will," said Dutton.

"Yep," said Havens. "That's why I figure I'll git my shots in while I still got the chance."

Stella's words continued to resonate in Tilden's head. *We've got to do something.* And he knew that he could not sit quietly any longer.

"Somebody else died last night," he said in a low, even voice.

Dutton had been chuckling. ". . . you and everybody else in town!"

"I said somebody else *died* last night. They found his body today." Tilden spoke evenly and louder this time.

Havens was giggling. "Yeah, how's that song go? 'Ain't no stoppin' us now,' right?"

"Aren't you two listening to me?" Tilden slapped his hands on the bar top, looked from one to the other, and waited until they both glared at him.

"Yeah, we heard you," said Dutton, his lower lip beginning to curl downward.

"Liebowitz is dead," said Tilden.

"Yeah, we heard," said Havens. "So what?"

"*So what*? How can you talk like that?" An icy needle of terror pierced his bowels.

Havens shrugged, grinned. "Talk's talk. It's cheap as shit. Besides, nobody ever liked Liebowitz—he was just a nasty old kike . . ."

Tilden leaned away from the bar. He wanted to be far from these men. It was as though they were suddenly emanating a killing stench, throwing off an aura of decay and corruption so foul that merely being close might be enough to become infected.

"Stella was right . . ." he said softly.

"What'd you say?" said Dutton. The butcher had grabbed the sleeve of Tilden's jacket and was twisting it in his fat grip.

"Don't you see what's *happening* here?" Tilden felt close to panic, but he forced himself to speak, to confront these two. "You all saw Liebowitz' face in the gallery last night, I *know* you did!"

Dutton chuckled softly. It was an obscene sound.

"Oh, yeah?" he asked. "And how do you know *that*?"

Another icy needle slid into Tilden's gut, pinning him like a wriggling bug to a piece of corkboard. The pain of admission bubbled up like dark bile. It filled his throat, trying to choke off his words, but he forced himself to speak.

"I know you saw him because . . . because *I* saw him, too, goddamn it! *I saw him, too*!" He choked off the final words and covered his eyes. "Oh, Jesus, help me . . . I saw him, too . . ."

Havens and Dutton looked at him with faces of stone. One of them put a hand on his shoulder.

"You know what, Mr. Strong? I think you are crackin' up, you know that? You know, like losin' your marbles?" Havens grinned as he lifted his cap and ran his fingers through dark, knotted thongs of hair. "I always did think you was a little queer, you know?"

Tilden looked at him as though in a daze. "What're you saying?"

"I'll tell you what he's sayin', Strong." Dutton moved his face close to Tilden's and spoke, his beery breath like a lethal fog. "Just because you own that grocery store and got your house already paid for and got that fruity son of yours going to one of them fancy schools back east, well it's like you always acted like you was *better* than the rest of us . . ."

"Yeah," said Havens. "Us *workin'* folks!"

"But I got news for you, Strong," said Dutton. "You ain't no better than nobody, and maybe you oughta remember that."

"I never— What do you mean?" Tilden felt confused, terrified.

Dutton chuckled sneeringly. "I mean you been standin' up to that counter takin' your shots just like everybody else in this damn town!"

Havens nodded. "So if I was you, I'd just shut my ugly face, huh?"

Dutton flowed off his barstool. "Come on, Havens . . . let's get the hell outa here."

"No, wait," said Tilden. "Wait, let me explain . . ."

"Fuck yer explainin'," said Havens. "We know all we need to know."

The smaller man dropped off his stool and moved to catch up with Dutton. Tilden watched them exit as the burning pain in his bowels grew more intense. What had he done? He had tried to do something, hadn't he? He should be feeling good, but if that was the case, then why was he feeling so bad?

He couldn't let them leave like that. Better to make them understand . . .

Fighting the influence of the two shots of bourbon, Tilden fled the womblike comfort of the bar. It was almost dark when he stepped out into the street.

CHAPTER 24

Stella paused on the front porch to compose herself.

She had to calm down. There was no sense getting upset because Mr. Strong would not help her, and she didn't want her aunt to see her in a distraught state of mind. Combined with the afterglow of emotional and sexual excitement she had experienced that day, everything threatened to overwhelm her. She was learning quickly that the world was far more complex than a child could ever imagine. If she did not maintain a rational view of all the new situations in her life, then they might indeed consume her.

Taking several deep breaths, she tried to relax. She looked out across the front lawn, up and down Sycamore Street. Neat hedges and painted picket fences, manicured grass and flower beds. It looked so serene, so peaceful in the waning light; it was difficult to imagine the deceit and self-loathing, the twisted feelings of hate and distrust which seethed like hungry maggots just beneath the surface of the town.

It was intriguing that she had never before thought of Brampton in such a dark light. Was this kind of cynicism also a part of growing up?

Stella shook her head slowly. Whatever was happening in Brampton was an eye-opener for her. For the first time, she was painfully aware of the duplicity of life, of how the nature of people could be so different, depending on how you looked at them.

This had been a time of changes, all right. In more ways than one.

Back under control, Stella entered the house and helped her aunt finish cooking their dinner. The two of them ate in relative silence, except when Aunt Leah probed her about her "tiff," as she called it, with Jamie. Thankfully, her aunt did not pursue the conversation when Stella glossed over the issue, claiming that everything was okay, and that it had not been a big deal in the first place.

Stella kept waiting for her aunt to mention the death of Mr. Liebowitz, but it never happened. That was odd because Aunt Leah was usually a walking obituary column. Stella could always tell when another town member's passing was about to be announced; her aunt would begin the conversation with: "Do you remember old Mrs. ———?" And after Stella usually said that she didn't know the person, Aunt Leah would sigh and shake her head with much drama, saying, "Well, she died . . ."

It was more than curious that Aunt Leah avoided mention of Mr. Liebowitz. She hadn't talked about Mr. Johannsen either.

Her aunt was no different from the rest of them. They were all trying to ignore everything.

Only Mr. Strong had suggested that he was aware

of the terrible things happening. But he was too scared to do anything about it.

As she began washing the dishes, Stella reflected upon her conversation with the grocer. The only good thing to have come out of it had been his confirmation about the faces. That meant that what had happened to Jamie was probably happening to everybody.

Everybody.

Stella wrinkled her shoulders at the thought, her muscles tightening involuntarily.

She noticed that her aunt had been in a hurry to clean up the dishes, and when her friends, three matronly women from her bridge club, came calling for their now-nightly trip to the meadow, Stella understood. Aunt Leah, like everyone else, had become hooked on the Magnificent Gallery. They were all addicted.

Reminding her to tend to her homework, Aunt Leah vanished into the evening amid the gay chatter of her friends. Stella knew that her mind was far too stimulated and agitated to even think about doing homework.

When she went up to her room, she called Jamie.

"I was just getting ready to call you," he said. "Nobody's here. They've all gone up to the meadow."

"I know the feeling."

"They wanted me to go," he said, "but I figured I'd go with you, if you wanted to."

"I don't know what I want to do, Jamie." She told him about the talk she had with Strong, how he confirmed the appearance of the victims' faces. Jamie didn't respond right away.

"Jamie, are you there?"

"Oh, yeah, I was just thinking . . ." He cleared his throat. "I can't stop thinking about this afternoon . . . with you . . . at the mill."

She smiled. She had expected that he would be preoccupied with what had happened. Laura Gleesinger had written that boys were more obsessed with sex than girls. They couldn't help it, the book had said; it was part of their raging body chemistry.

"I know, Jamie," she said softly, almost motherly. "It's all right. I understand."

"You do?" He sounded more than a little surprised.

"I think so." She paused, drew a breath. "Jamie, it was beautiful."

"I was hoping you weren't getting a case of the guilts," he said. "And I don't want you to think I was trying to cop a feel for the hell of it. It was a really beautiful thing we shared, Stella."

"Don't be so worried about me," she said. "I know you really care, Jamie."

"Okay, just checking . . ."

"Besides, we need something good, something beautiful right about now."

"Huh?"

"There isn't much else in this town we can be very happy about." She told him how her aunt had completely avoided mentioning Liebowitz' death.

"Yeah, I know what you mean. My mother acted like nothing was the matter," he said. "What do you think we should do?"

"I don't know. I want to stay as far away from that meadow as I can, but that won't help matters any. We've got to go out there, Jamie."

"Stella, I don't mind telling you—that place is creepy. I keep thinking of what it was like when I was shooting . . . It's hard to explain, but there's a part of me that wants to try it again."

"You don't have to try to explain. I know what you're saying. I'm glad I haven't tried it, though I *am* curious to know what it's like."

"No, Stella. Don't even *think* about trying it," said Jamie, his voice rising in panic. "You don't want to know, believe me!"

"It might be the only way to understand what's going on. How are we going to try to stop Magister if we don't know what we're up against?"

Jamie paused. "I don't know, Stella. Maybe we're kidding ourselves."

"What do you mean?"

"I mean maybe there isn't any way to stop this thing. Have you ever thought about that?"

The question pierced her deeply. It was a possibility she had tried not to consider. "Yes," she said after a pause. "I've thought about it. But I don't believe it. That's too pessimistic for me, Jamie. I just can't think like that. There's *got* to be something we can do. Besides, if there isn't, we might as well just kill ourselves."

"Well, we could maybe run away," he said. "Go somewhere else."

"We'd be running away from ourselves. No, that wouldn't solve anything. We've got to face this Mister Magister and find out why he's doing this to everybody."

"I guess that means you want to go to the meadow tonight?"

"Jamie, I don't think we have much choice."

"Okay, I'll be over in a few minutes."

* * *

Moonlight filtered through the trees, casting lace-like patterns on the streets and rooftops. Stella followed Jamie from one pool of lamppost light to the next as they pedaled up Madison to Center Street. The main street of Brampton looked desolate and forgotten. It was scary to see everything so empty and dead.

Jamie turned east on Center and glided toward the edge of town. He looked back at her every once in a while to ensure that she was following him, and she was grateful for his thoughtfulness. The nights were getting progressively cooler, and soon it would be too chilly to fight the bracing wind of nighttime bike rides. Even now, Stella's scalp felt cold from the combs of cool air which parted her long hair as she rode. The meadow and the crowds loomed ahead.

When they arrived, cycling past the long lines of parked cars and pickups and vans, they remained on the outskirts of the crowd. Jamie locked their tenspeeds together and chained them to a double trunk of white birch.

"Let's just stay back here and watch for a while," said Stella.

"What're you looking for?" asked Jamie as they stood under the cover of the birch trees.

"I don't know yet. Do you see Magister?"

Jamie scanned the area for a moment.

"No. That's weird. He's usually hanging around somewhere."

"Maybe he's out getting his latest victim," said Stella in a whisper.

"No, wait! There he is, over on the other side of the wagon. He's trading in his jar full of quarters for an empty one. Jeez, he must be making a fortune out here."

Stella followed his pointing finger, and the crowd parted for an instant, allowing her to see the tall, scarecrow-thin figure of the carnival man. His droopy-brimmed hat concealed most of his face, but even from this distance she could see the long, gaunt line of his jaw, the knifeslice of his mouth. Just as he tilted his head, appearing to look up at her through the aperture in the mass of bodies, the moment passed and the gap closed.

"I don't think he really cares about the money," said Stella.

"Yeah, you're probably right about that."

Neither of them spoke for a while. Stella studied the crowd, nodding as she recognized familiar faces. They moved about the clearing as though following some mystically choreographed pattern. No one seemed impatient or surly as they slipped in and out of the lines which led to places at the gallery.

Couldn't they see what they were doing? Didn't any of them feel the danger of Magister?

The questions were the same ones which had been stalking her logic and her emotions since the wagon first appeared. If there were answers, she had not yet come upon them, and her feelings of helplessness were still growing. It would be so easy to just give up, to give in and forget.

"Hey!" said Jamie, pointing across the road at an approaching vehicle. "Look who's coming!"

It was a big, stylish, heavy American luxury car. Its polished dark maroon surface reflected the light of the moon and the colored bulbs in the trees as it crunched along the gravel and ground to a stop.

Stella watched as Mr. Strong jumped out from behind the wheel and moved quickly toward the crowd and the wagon.

"He looks like he's in a big hurry," said Jamie.

"He looks like he's really upset, too," she said, and she wondered if her talk with the grocer had rallied him into taking charge. Oh, God, she hoped so. She would need allies, for somehow she knew that eventually she would have to confront the evil which had come to her town.

"Where is he going?" asked Jamie. "Looks like he's looking for somebody."

"Magister?"

Jamie shook his head. "I don't think so. You can't miss *him.*"

She touched his sleeve and he reacted by moving closer, putting his arm around her. She felt immediately warmer. "Jamie, let's get closer. Let's see what Mr. Strong is doing."

"Okay."

He took her hand and they moved forward, blending in with the crowd. They were slowed by the many greetings from people who knew them, especially from several cliques from school, who had finally noticed that she and Jamie were "involved." Stella tried her best to ignore the banter which sparked around them, keeping her eyes on Tilden Strong, who had assumed a more frantic look the deeper he pushed into the crowd.

Stella watched as Mr. Strong weaved his way between the crush of bodies near the open end of the shooting gallery. He approached Mr. Dutton and Sam Havens, who were standing near the front of the line, waiting to take their turns.

"What does he want with *those* two?" asked Jamie, still easing them through the crowd. It was his intention to get as close to Mr. Strong as possible.

The grocer, garbed in dress slacks and a white shirt, a bow tie and a gray cardigan golf sweater, looked harried. He reached out and grabbed Mr. Dutton's sleeve, and the large, fleshy man wheeled on him like a cornered rat.

CHAPTER 25

"Hey, what the hell're you *doin'*?" The jowled, moon-face of Joseph Dutton glowed a florid scarlet as he slurred his words at Tilden Strong. Initially, he did not seem to recognize whom he was talking to, but seemed to be merely reacting to what he assumed was an attack.

Tilden had never really looked into Dutton's face so clearly, so intently before. Unshaven, rimmed with a patina of sweat and grime, the butcher was a truly unsavory-looking, ugly man. It was an aspect not improved by the sneering quality of his mouth and the pinched, squinty look to his bird-shot eyes. But that didn't really matter now. Tilden had to talk to Dutton and Havens.

"Excuse me," he said. "I just wanted to explain what I was talking about back there . . ."

The hard, small, round eyes focused, and Dutton started laughing. He nudged Havens, who was rubbernecking at some nearby high school girls. "Hey, Sam . . . look who's here!"

Sam turned slowly, his head rotating like the turret of a battle tank. A grin sliced into the bottom of his face and he started cackling, an odd kind of giggle which made his Adam's apple bob up and down like a buoy on choppy seas.

"Hey, it's the groceryman!" said Havens. "Come down to take a few shots, did you?"

Dutton and Havens both erupted into laughter. Tilden felt his face turning red. He didn't like the idea of being the butt of jokes in public.

It reminded him of his grammar school days, when he had been an outcast for being a "brain," for always knowing the answers when the teachers called his name, for wearing his pants cinched up under his rib cage, for wearing a crewcut when everyone else was greasing their hair into pompadours and spitcurls. He couldn't count the number of times he had been surrounded by taunting crowds on the school playground. He could feel the radiating heat of their staring eyes, the sting of their under-the-breath jeers.

He could feel it then, just as he was beginning to feel it now.

"Havens, I need to talk to you," he said. Then, looking at Dutton: "Both of you."

"I think you've said more than enough," said Dutton.

"No, listen, please . . ." Tilden could feel his voice rising in pitch. There was the beginning of a quaver in his throat, and he loathed the way he was starting to sound. "Was thinking about what I said to you back in the bar, and, well, maybe I was wrong . . ."

"Maybe you was," said Havens.

"Hey, it don't matter anyway," said Dutton. "We don't care one way or another, you just lost your nerve, that's all. And when a man loses his nerve, it's as plain as the nose on his face. You don't have to explain nothin'."

"I'm not trying to 'explain' anything," said Tilden, suddenly growing more afraid of these men than he had ever previously been. "I just want you to know that I meant no harm by what I was saying back there. I just wanted to see what you thought, that's all."

"Well, you found out what we thought, didn't you?" said Havens, still grinning.

Dutton chuckled. "Listen, Strong, why don't you just get out of here, all right? We're out to have us some fun, and we don't particularly like you comin' up here and spoilin' it for us, okay?"

Tilden looked at the overweight, slovenly man who was sneering down at him. A chill ran down his back as he realized that he was only making a bigger fool of himself by trying to reason with them. Either they were beyond reason or they had never possessed it in the first place. These men were dangerous, and as the truth of it sank home, Tilden felt a new wave of horror crash over him, bending him over, folding him in upon himself, and threatening to subsume him into the pit of his fears.

He could feel the attention of the crowd focusing upon their confrontation. All ambient noise settled away like dust as everyone began watching and listening. Tilden could feel his skin crawling under the intensity of the crowd's gaze.

"Wait," he said. "Let me just—"

Two spaces opened up at the counter. Havens moved away from Tilden, heading toward the wagon.

"Hey! Let's go, Joe," he said, motioning to his comrade.

Dutton brushed past Tilden and leaned his weight upon the counter. He and Havens dropped quarters into the Mason jar, picked up their rifles, and took aim into the darkness.

Looking back, Tilden could sense the crowd watching him, wondering what he might do next. The leading edge of the crowd drew tighter around the gallery, encircling Tilden, walling him in, like a prisoner on view for their pleasure. A claustrophobic pressure was building in him; he needed to get away from this place. There was a pervasive sense of evil emanating from the crowd. It was like the foulness of decay, and he imagined that the Christians, when thrown to the lions, might have detected a similar stench from the stands of the Colosseum.

Suddenly, Havens burst into cackling, then hooting laughter. Tilden turned to see the skinny little man nudging Joseph Dutton, then lean close to speak into his ear.

"Hey, Joe . . . take a look at this, will you?"

Havens pointed into the blackest heart of the gallery.

Dutton looked for a moment, then chuckled darkly. "Well, ain't that something . . . ?"

What the hell was going on? Tilden looked back at the crowd. They seemed to be waiting to see how the small drama would unfold. He wheeled back toward the gallery and moved in upon the men at the counter.

Dutton and Havens were laughing as they aimed and fired into the night-sky depths of the gallery.

Wedging in between them, Tilden tried to see into the darkness.

"What are you two laughing at? What are you doing?"

"Hey, watch it!" said Havens, who continued to fire into the steady procession of targets.

Tilden looked over the man's shoulder and felt the hypnotic effect of the target display attempt to draw him in. Watching intently, he saw the clownish faces leering and gaping, flaring as they were touched by tracer beams and banished to oblivion. He saw why they had been laughing.

He saw his own face in the darkness.

No!

It couldn't be possible . . . and yet it was.

Elongated, hyperbolic, almost a caricature, the image of Tilden Strong kept appearing, vanishing, and reappearing in the endless depths of the gallery. Each time his face appeared, Havens and Dutton would burst into childish, whooping laughter and concentrate their fire at the image.

Each time, his face vanished before sustaining a direct hit, but it was only a matter of time.

God, no! *No!*

Grabbing Havens' arm, Tilden tried to pull the man's grip away from the rifle, to distract him, to stop him. He had to stop both of them!

"Sam, cut it out! Stop! Please, stop, you've got to stop doing this!"

Moving quickly, Havens twisted out of Tilden's grip. His lips were curled back in a wolfish snarl as he spoke. "Keep your filthy hands offa me! You hear?! Get the fuck offa me, you asshole!" He pushed Tilden away roughly.

Panicked, almost falling, Tilden reached out blindly and caught Dutton's arm. It was a fleshy column of strength which supported his weight. Tilden yanked downward, disrupting the butcher's aim.

"Dutton, please . . . no! Please. You've got to

stop this! Don't you know what you're doing? Oh, God, you've got to stop!"

Dutton swung around like a grizzly bear surprised in its own den. Raising a big hamlike hand, he backhanded Tilden under the jaw, almost lifting him out of his shoes with the impact.

Light flickered before Tilden's eyes as he fell backward.

"You get the hell away from here!" yelled Dutton. The sound of his voice seemed distant and faint as Tilden fell an impossibly long way to the earth. The crowd had erupted into laughter before he hit the ground.

As in a nightmare, his vision pinwheeled, and the faces of the crowd spun into a mocking, vicious blur. He had to get away. To get as far away as he could from whatever had overtaken everyone.

Scrabbling in the dirt, trying to get to his feet, he must have looked like a buffoon. The crowd burst into a new round of laughter, and as he stood up, he saw Havens and Dutton at the counter, grinning down at him.

"Can you believe it?" asked Havens. "And all for the price of a quarter!"

Tilden watched as the two men chuckled, then turned back to shoot into the gallery.

After that, things became confused.

Tilden Strong had only brief, lucid moments as panic fully overtook him. He pushed his way through the crowd to the sound of someone screaming.

He did not at first realize that it was his own voice.

Running, stumbling, out of breath, he ran away from the meadow. He ran away from the town and into the harvested cornfields north of the highway.

Ahead, hanging against the sky and frosted with moonlight, the specterlike figure of a scarecrow awaited him.

Tilden ran past it, and into the empty darkness.

CHAPTER 26

Backing away from the edge of the crowd, Stella moved as though in a trance. The mocking laughter of the crowd still echoed in her mind, and the movie screen in her head kept replaying the scene of poor Mr. Strong stumbling and falling away from the gallery, from the vicious jeers of the townspeople. She could see the look of abject terror on his face as he shrank away from them.

Stella understood that terror well. She could feel the evil coming off the crowd like waves of heat. It was a low, wretched emanation, like the surly stench of a mob which has gathered for a taste of blood. It was the smell of death. She was afraid to breathe it in for fear of becoming infected with the same lethal germ which transformed the whole town.

"Stella, where're you going?"

Jamie's voice intruded on her thoughts as she unconsciously retreated from the mob. She needed to get away so she could think straight. She'd forgotten about Jamie. Looking back, she saw him jogging to keep up with her.

She must have been running, without realizing it. Stella slowed once she was free of the crowd, then stopped on the shoulder of the road and waited for Jamie.

"Hey, are you all right?" he asked as he moved close to her.

"Jamie, that was horrible. Did you see them? Could you feel it?"

"You mean Mr. Dutton and Sam Havens?"

"Not just them . . ." She described her feelings in the crowd, how she could sense the hate in its collective heart.

Jamie nodded, but she wasn't certain he'd understood. She looked back toward the gallery and noticed that Mister Magister was no longer hovering near the counter. He had slipped into the shadows and could be anywhere. The thought of the strange man, if he was indeed a man, lurking in the darkness beyond the meadow began to prey upon her.

"What're you looking for?" asked Jamie.

"Magister's not there. He disappeared again."

"Did you see the way Mr. Strong freaked out? I couldn't believe it," said Jamie.

"It was horrible. I've never seen anything so awful."

"I know what freaked him out, I'll bet."

Stella looked at him. "You mean when he looked in the gallery?"

Jamie nodded. "Sure. I bet he saw his *own* face."

"I know. I had the same feeling. It was terrible," she said. "Did you see how terrified he looked?"

Jamie chuckled nervously. "Wouldn't *you* be scared if you saw your face in there?"

Stella could only nod. She wanted to talk, but no

words would come. She could hear the idiot hum of the crowd, not far away. It was a mindless sound, like the droning whisper of a hive. She had to get away from this place, away from the crowd whose aura hung over the meadow like a heavy, poisonous cloud.

"Stella, are you okay?" Jamie moved closer to her, touched her arm.

She looked at him, all dark eyes and dark hair, and sharply chiseled cheekbones. He would someday be a handsome man, but in the moonlight he looked very much a boy this night.

"Stella . . . ?"

She hunched her shoulders as a chill caressed her. "I don't know," she said finally. "I don't know what to do."

"I think we should get out of here," he said.

Jamie was right. There was nothing they could do here, tonight. She could feel an overwhelming energy in the air, as though the crowd had generated a static pulse and it was making the air itself sing with charged particles. It felt like a too-dry summer evening right before a terrible electrical storm.

But it wasn't right to just turn their heads and run from the danger and the evil that were thriving there. It was growing stronger, she could feel it. She didn't know what to do. Maybe Jamie was right.

She was about to answer him when she felt someone looking at her. As light as a dragonfly's wing, but no less real, she detected the invisible *presence* of eyes, watching her.

Turning quickly, she looked off into the darkness of the open cornfields, in the direction where Mr. Strong had disappeared. And there, just beyond the reach of the glow from the colored lights, she saw him.

His face was long and sunken, gaunt and pale beneath his black hat—almost skullish with its angles and planed edges. Only his eyes gave Mister Magister the look of life; they burned with an intensity which could surely wither any who tried to stand against them.

Jamie caught her staring into the shadows, and following her gaze, saw the thin, tall shape of the carnival man watching them.

"Stella, he's right there," said Jamie in a hoarse whisper.

She nodded, but could not speak.

Grabbing her by the arm, Jamie guided her quickly to the white birches where he'd chained the ten-speeds. She stood as though hypnotized while Jamie rattled the lock and chain off the bike frames. Stella could not break eye contact with the dark man. Her heartbeat had accelerated and the sound of the crowd had slipped away, fading like the sound of the sea in a conch shell. She could feel the fear building in Jamie as he straddled his bike, hunched down over the handlebars.

"Come on, Stella!"

Who are you? she thought. What are you doing to us?

She wanted so badly to confront Magister with these questions, and she could almost feel the dark man reaching out to her with an invisible gesture, motioning her to stay, to join him. Magister stood back, remaining in the shadows. He made no threatening move toward them, and she knew that she should stay, but Jamie had not released his grip upon her arm, and she could hear the heavy pant of his breath.

"Stella! Come on, let's go!"

Turning away from the shadows, she felt the contact break.

Automatically, she mounted her bike and began pedaling. Jamie, leaning into the night, had already rushed out onto the blacktop, heading for the false sanctuary of the town.

CHAPTER 27

It had been quite an evening, thought Magister impassively. These people were as dramatic as they were demonstrative in their choices. It had been many measures of time since he had witnessed a display of such irony and swift resolution. The mood of the crowd, its collective attitude, and its *animus* seemed to be assuming its final shape and texture, hardening into a carapace which would prove impenetrable to any human feeling.

It was an accretive, geometric process, a societal architecture which he had seen before, in other times, on other worlds. And even though it always displayed a new outward design, it was always supported by the same basic superstructure, the same underlying girders and struts of hate and fear and self-loathing.

How endlessly fascinating. How utterly perverse was the process, which once started was so rarely halted.

He looked out at the crowd and could feel its energy waning. Like a nocturnal predator, it had spent itself and now, sated, was slipping into lassitude. Soon the crowd would slink off into the town to sleep off the torpor which was overtaking it. But by the next evening, the process would begin again, and he would be waiting for them.

That was the way it worked. He would be waiting for them, as long as they required him.

They could not know that their insane little game would not stop here, in this insignificant little town. They could not know that the cancerous growth they now cultivated would spread across the land, ignoring all human-made boundaries, until the entire world, the entire species, was infected with the final entropy of the spirit.

He nodded to himself, accepting their fate. He had been traveling a metaphysical road since the beginning of forever, and he would always do so. There would always be new worlds and new peoples who cried out to be tested.

Turning away from the crowd, he looked again to the copse of white birch trees where the young girl had been standing.

Although he did not have human emotions, Magister felt what could only be called disappointment. When he saw the girl vanish into the night, her fear trailing behind her like a dark banner, he was saddened. Her presence in the midst of the others was like a bright beacon on a storm-ravaged coast, and her departure left a darkening pall over the meadow and its counterfeit merriment.

As he stood watching her dwindle into the distance, he wondered what would have happened if she had remained, if she had eventually stepped up to his counter.

Would there have been different effects? Would she have succumbed quite so easily?

But these questions were secondary.

As the crowd began to dissipate like the smoke which clings to a battlefield, Magister wondered if she would return.

CHAPTER 28

"Good night, Stella," said Jamie.

He had his arms around her as they stood under the cover of the front porch. His breath was sweet and fresh as it mingled with her own. He kissed her with a gentleness that communicated his feelings beautifully. At any other time, she would have reciprocated with a hug and a kiss of her own, but tonight she was too distracted.

"Be careful, Jamie," she said.

He released her, stepped back, and looked into her eyes.

"What's wrong? Did I do something wrong?"

She forced herself to smile. "No, of course not. It's not you. I just can't get that scene out of my mind. I keep thinking about poor Mr. Strong."

Jamie nodded but said nothing. Nervously he looked over his shoulder, out toward Madison Street. The neighborhood was as quiet and dark as a ghost town. They were literally alone on the entire street.

"It's so quiet . . ." he said finally.

"They're all still out there," she said.

"It's getting late. They should be coming back soon." He kissed her again, this time just a little more than a ginger peck. "Well, I guess I better get home. You don't want me to come in, do you?"

"I do, but my aunt might get upset if she found us together. You better not."

Jamie grinned. "Yeah, okay. You want me to walk you to school tomorrow morning?"

"That'll be good," she said, but as dark and quiet as it seemed right now, she wondered if the morning would ever come.

Jamie stepped back, holding her hand for a moment. "You go on in," he said. "I'll leave after I know you're safe inside."

She nodded and slipped her key into the lock, pushed open the heavy oak door with the stained-glass inserts.

"Good night, Jamie."

Closing the door, she listened for his footsteps as he shuffled down the steps and walked slowly out to the treelined sidewalk. The moon was high in the sky now, and slipping through the cloud cover, its light washed over the lawns and hedges like spilled milk.

The hall chandelier cast long shadows up the stairs, but Stella was not afraid of ascending to the dark landing. As she went up to her room, she kept fighting off the feeling that she should not have run away tonight. She felt as though by running, she had turned her back on the whole town.

Turning on the little lamp by her bed, she picked up her journal and a pen. Maybe it would be better if she could try to compose her thoughts. It always seemed to help if she could get things down on paper. Her captured feelings and ideas always made more sense when she could examine them like that.

But there was so much to think about, so much to deal with.

In addition to everything else, there was the growing awareness of her coming womanhood, of her sexual desires and her emotional needs. Because of Magister, she felt that she had been ignoring these new aspects of her self. But they remained within her, surging beneath the surface of her mind like a dark, mysterious current. It was a wellspring of new sensations, into which she sometimes wished she might plunge without fear or forethought. But at other times she wanted to be cautious.

She worried about her feelings, and how some would construe them as "sinful" or "wicked." Despite the sermons of Father Doheny, Stella could not accept that. To deny the natural order of things was absurd, and sex was a part of the natural order. Could Nature have any concept of morality? She doubted it.

And how could such feelings of love and gentle giving be sinful in the first place? What could be wrong in wanting to share and give to another?

Sometimes, when she thought too much about these things, she became more muddled, more confused. She knew that she was entering a new phase of her life, and each step forward was a struggle. She was passing through a place where issues and meanings lay wrapped in a curious mist, an obscuring scrim of mystery and doubt.

The appearance of Magister and his Magnificent Gallery only complicated the issues.

Why was she the only one to really see the cause and effect of his presence among them? She knew that Jamie agreed with her, stood by her, but she wondered if he would have done so on his own. Was it only his love for her, his fear of losing her, which kept him from again leaning into the darkness of the gallery?

She knew there were no answers to these questions, but she could not keep from asking them, from allowing them to repeat over and over in her mind.

As she sat in the small pool of lamplight, carefully transcribing her thoughts, wording everything as clearly as possible, she heard sounds on the first floor. It was Aunt Leah returning, padding softly about the house, preparing for bed as quietly as she could. Stella felt a sense of relief pass over her, knowing that her aunt was safely home, that the evening at the meadow had come to an end at last.

But thoughts of the meadow made her think of Mr. Strong shambling off into the dark fields, his face a ragged mask of terror. It made her think of the carnival man, finally alone with his jars of quarters and his magic wagon, somehow claiming dominion over this small town. It made her realize how alone she was.

Despite the lateness of the hour, she knew there was no way she would sleep tonight.

She must go back there.

The thought broke the surface of her mind, shattering any last notions of complacency or doubt. She had to face the object of her fear. Stella knew that if she continued to do nothing, she would become like the rest; she would eventually be consumed by whatever it was that had taken over the town.

Closing her journal, she listened for any sounds that would indicate that her aunt was still awake and, hearing nothing, she slipped carefully down the back stairs to the kitchen. She left by the back door in almost total silence, and walked her ten-speed all the way down the driveway to the street before mounting and pedaling off.

The cloud cover had broken up completely now, and the full moon's glare illuminated the streets with a false dawn. Stella had never been out so late, and there was an odd excitement in it. She felt a freedom she'd never experienced before. No one knew she was out there. She sensed a sudden, brief giddiness, which gave her the feeling that she could do *anything,* and no one would ever find out. She was like a thief in the night as she glided silently past darkened houses and shuttered windows.

Reaching Center Street, finding it bathed in the cool lunar light, she was amazed at how quiet and empty the middle of the town now seemed. There surely existed another world, another dimension, during these dark and silent hours. It was like seeing everything as though in a dream.

And then she was free of the town, moving quickly through the bracing night air along the state highway. The meadow loomed ahead, now deserted except for the unimposing bulk of the carnival wagon, its wheels caressed by subtle fingers of ground fog.

Stella coasted to a stop and lay her bike in the grassy verge by the shoulder. Standing rigid for an instant, she listened to the ratchet songs of the crickets and the cries of foraging night birds. There was no other sound. If Magister was still by his wagon, he also made no sound.

She took several steps forward, then stopped again to listen. Even the crickets had stopped their chirping, and the wind which rustled dry stalks in the cornfields had also died. It was as though each step closer to the wagon took her deeper into a pit which absorbed all sounds, swallowing them up forever.

There was an eeriness about the place, a feeling of otherworldliness, of alienness, a final warning to flee.

But she had come this far, and she knew there was no turning back.

Increasing her stride, Stella walked straight to the wagon, which hulked in the moon shadows like an abandoned pillbox on a Normandy beach. Its rear counter was still unhinged, the rifles bleaching in the milky light. She moved to the edge of the counter and fought off an urge to touch the stock of the nearest weapon. Instead her gaze leaped into the gallery itself, and for a moment, her breath seized up in her breast.

Looking into the wagon was like looking into the Pit, into the bottomless abyss that must be Hell itself. All sense of direction and position lost meaning. There was a feeling of total *nothingness*, a complete absence of light and form. It was like staring into the eye of a black hole, into a wound punched into the belly of the universe, beyond which not even the cold, dead stone of the final entropy could lie.

Stella fought off a dizzying, vertiginous sensation, and forced herself to look away from the opening.

Into the eyes of Mister Magister.

He was standing behind the wagon, half-consumed by shadows. He could have been there all along, or he might have just taken form from the snippets of fog which snaked and tendriled close to the earth.

"So, you have returned." His voice was deep and

resonant, his words perfectly pronounced, as though prepared in advance and machined on a broadcaster's lathe. Up close, he was taller than she had imagined, but still terribly thin. His cape was fastened by a piece of silver which glinted in the moonlight. She could see it clearly: a skeletal claw encircling a globe.

She looked at him, and waited for him to continue, and when he did not, she heard herself speaking, as though listening to someone else.

"I know you," she said. And that was odd, because until that very moment, she could not remember consciously identifying him. But suddenly, in his presence, it was bubbling out of her. "I know who you are . . ."

"You do?" He sounded mildly surprised.

"You're the Reaper."

Magister chuckled softly, stepped forward so that he was within arm's reach of her. She half-expected that he would change now. With his identity revealed, he would transform before her eyes. The pale flesh would melt away and she would stare into the eternity of eyeless sockets, the obscene grin of his naked jaws.

"You are, aren't you?" she said. "The one they call the Grim Reaper."

"And who is that?" he asked in a silky, gentle voice.

"Death."

Magister half-smiled. "No, child. I am not . . . that one."

Stella fought the urge to back away from him. He was looking down at her with an odd, almost patronizing grin.

"Then who are you?" she said loudly, noticing

how the meadow seemed to swallow up her voice. "The Dark Angel? Are you *Satan*?"

Magister touched his hand to the counter, slapped the oak panel loudly. "No, young one. I am not a myth from the minds of fearful men. Do not confuse me with your legends. I am *real*."

"Then who are you? What do you want with us?"

Magister sighed. A very human sigh. "It does not matter who I am. Know only that I have come from a faraway place. A place beyond the imaginings of men."

He was telling her nothing, and she wondered how long he would allow her to badger him. She needed answers.

"But what do you want with us? And why are you killing us?" She asked the questions quickly, then stepped back away from the gallery, afraid to look into its depths, not knowing how he might react after being so blatantly accused of his crimes.

"I kill no one," he said. "You are killing yourselves."

The words pierced her deeply. She knew what he meant, knew he was painfully correct.

"It's all so crazy—you coming here and all this happening," she said. "We wouldn't be killing anybody if it wasn't for you and your gallery!"

"You are wrong, child."

"What do you mean?"

Magister gestured toward the town with a graceful sweep of his arm. "It seems to me that your town was killing those who died long before I came, only they were doing it much more *slowly*."

Stella could only nod her head, understanding his implicit meaning. This Magister was much more than a carnival man. His words were couched in metaphor

and portent. There was an eerie drama about him
which was hypnotic, almost appealing.

"You understand me, don't you?" he asked.

"Oh, yes," said Stella. "I certainly do."

"And do you agree?"

She nodded her head. "Yes, I do. Even though it
hurts to admit it, I think you're right."

She looked at him, waiting for him to respond, but
he only looked at her with a curious, unreadable
expression. He seemed content to stand there, looking at her indefinitely. It was unsettling to stare at
one another in the silence. She much preferred when
they were talking.

"How long will you let this go on?" she said
finally, the first shades of desperation coloring her
words.

Magister sighed softly, shook his head very slowly.
He looked away as though embarrassed, then back
at her.

"I don't know," he said. "I'm afraid it could go on
for a long, long time . . ."

"But what happens when . . ." She fumbled for
the right words, and failing, pushed ahead anyway.
"What happens when we run out of scapegoats?"

Magister looked at her with renewed interest.
"Scapegoats?"

"You know—the outcasts, the ones that nobody
likes. That's how it works, doesn't it?" Stella could
feel her heart beating wildly in her chest. What was
happening to her?

"You tell me," he said. "*Is* that how it works?"

She nodded. "I think so, yes."

Magister nodded, his face an unreadable mask.

"Well, what happens when the outcasts are all
gone?" she cried. "What then? Do we start in on our

neighbors, our friends? Cousins and brothers and sisters? Even our parents? Our *children*?"

Magister nodded. "It could come to that, yes."

She wanted to cry, but something in her held it in check. It was as though she stood before an enormous engine, a malevolent machine which, once set running, would rattle and bang and shake until it destroyed itself in a vibrating frenzy. The machine was what had once been the basic humanity of her town, and she wanted to find the off switch, wanted to shut it down before it was too late. But she felt helpless and insignificant before the great machine. Did she wish for the impossible? Could it really come down to such an end?

Suddenly her pain was replaced by anger and she glared at the pale, thin man. "You'll let it go on forever, won't you? You'll never stop it!"

"Child, know this: I *cannot* stop it."

"What?"

Magister nodded. "It is not my decision to stop this thing. My task is to only set the wheel in motion."

"Oh, my God . . ." she said, feeling another wave of despair curl over her.

"I am only a tool," said Magister. "I am a means to an end."

"You mean it cannot be stopped?" Stella looked away, back toward the town where everyone slept the sleep of the righteous and the innocent. She almost laughed at the lie of that old cliché.

"I did not say that," he said softly.

"Then it *can* be stopped? Oh, Magister, tell me . . . How can we stop it?"

He shook his head, looked away for a moment. "I am sorry, but I cannot instruct you in this."

How frustrating this was! She felt as though she were playing an elaborate game with him, as if there were certain protocols to be followed—but no one had given her the rules.

"You make it sound so hopeless," she said.

"No, not really. Believe me when I say that it is not hopeless." Magister paused, looked into the gallery, then back into Stella's eyes. "Your being here, confronting me, is proof that there is still hope."

Stella tried to break the bond of his penetrating gaze, but could not. She tried to speak, but found no words.

"Here," said Magister, gesturing toward the interior of his wagon. "Come here and look inside. Perhaps then you will understand what you are up against."

How could he even *think* she could do such a thing! She had seen the faraway looks in the eyes of the others who peered into the gallery. Even Jamie. Even he had been yoked under its power.

"No!" she cried, backing up a step. "Never! You won't get me that easily!"

Magister smiled graciously, almost bowed. "No, you don't understand. I don't want to *get* you. I only want you to realize what forces are at work here."

He gestured again toward the open end of the wagon, which lay exposed to the night like a blood-dark wound, a total *absence* of light.

"No," she said. "You can't make me do it."

He nodded. "True. I can only ask."

She was taken up short by his simple reply. There was something gentle in his voice, something which belied the sinister aspects of his appearance. She felt he at least deserved a reply. "Jamie told me what it was like to look in there. I don't want to be hooked like everybody else."

Magister enacted a knowing grin. "I don't think you could be 'hooked' in any case, but know this: It is not the gallery I ask you to gaze upon."

"Well, what is it, then?"

"The gallery is gone for the evening," he said, stepping closer to the dark opening, glancing for a moment into its depths, then back at Stella. "This is now a portal, a window . . ."

Was he trying to trick her? "A window?" she asked. "To what?"

"To the soul of the night," said Magister. "To the heart of the heart of the cosmos. Come, come gaze upon it."

Such eloquent words, thought Stella, wondering how much truth lay within them. She inched forward, then stepped back. Would he try to trick her? Hurt her? Kill her the way he had so obviously killed the others?

"Is this a trick?" she asked in a voice no louder than the whisper of brittle leaves.

"No trick."

Stella drew in a breath, then exhaled slowly. Looking at the open maw of the wagon, she slowly moved forward again. She dared not glance at Magister, preferring to fix her gaze upon the open end of the gallery. As she drew closer, a feeling of solemnity settled upon her, as though she were entering a cathedral or a shrine. The open end of the wagon awaited her.

She turned and faced the darkness. It was like standing on the edge of the world, on the edge of a pit which fell away from reality with a headlong rush and opened into a vast, starry abyss. There was a sense of motion, of leaping forward, as though she peered through the window of a great ship that plowed through the night. Globular clusters floated and turned like snowflakes. The luminescence of stellar nebulae burned with hot color as they drifted past, and the great, pinwheeling motion of spiral galaxies rolled past her viewpoint in all directions like coins tossed carelessly from a king's carriage. It was a dizzying experience, an endless rush to the heart of creation, a heart which she knew could never be reached, which would forever lie beyond the farthest shoals of night.

And then she was aware of the silence. It was not an ordinary silence, a mere lack of sound. It was much more than that. It was Silence. The sound of the nothingness between the worlds. The perfect vacuum of the universe, silence in the vast sea of darkness in which whole galaxies could fall screaming into a monstrous black hole without a sound; a silence in which an ancient star might explode in brilliant, supernoval death, and utter not even a whimper.

Stella continued to stare into the endless play of light and shadow, of being and nothingness. If this was a display of Magister's power, she knew she was defeated. What she witnessed was no trick, no carnival illusion. It was *real*, and the acceptance of this made her eyes tear with stinging salt.

What was this gallery? This man? If he really *was* a man.

Even as she formed the questions in her mind, she knew the answers. The longer she stared into the window, the more she understood. It was just as he'd said. She knew now that Magister was only part of a larger mechanism, that he was not the real power. There was something infinitely more grand behind it all.

Stella gazed onward, drinking in the endless spill of cosmic life. She stared into the heart of the universe and found it to be a cold, indifferent place. It was a monstrous piece of machinery, grinding down toward a faraway heat-death, laboring beyond the boundaries of good and evil.

She stared into the heart of the cosmos and discovered that it had no heart at all.

Turning away from the gallery was an effortless thing. Magister had not lied.

He stood watching her.

"You are only part of it, aren't you?" she said.

Magister nodded.

"It all seems so meaningless when you look in there."

"Yes," said Magister. "But I suspect you do not believe that."

"At first I thought it was a terrible evil that had come to us," said Stella. "But now I know there's something worse."

Magister nodded.

"How can we go up against something like that? How can anything stop such a force?" She was almost in tears now, and she could feel their salty sting building up in the corners of her eyes. "Oh, God, I want it to *stop*, I really do."

The gaunt face regarded her with gathering interest.

"Yes, you do," he said. "I can sense it."

She looked at him as a new idea touched her, as the first tear broke free and ran down her cheek.

"Wait," she said. "If it can be stopped, then we must stop it ourselves. That's it, isn't it?"

"Yes, that is part of the process."

"But *how*?"

Magister paused, deep in thought. Then: "Tell me child, do you hate your people for what they are doing?"

She was taken aback by the question, but she replied almost immediately. "Hate them? Of course not! I *care* about them. They're just afraid, that's all. Even if they do realize what they're doing, they can't stop, because they're *afraid*. No, Magister, I don't hate them."

He nodded his head slowly. "I see . . ."

"They don't understand. You've got to forgive them, Magister."

"It is not my place to forgive," he said. "It is *you* who must do that."

"I *do* forgive them!" She almost yelled out the words, and her voice seemed to echo across the open fields, breaking loose from the blanketlike confines of the meadow. "I want to help them. I want to help all of us. I care, and I want it to stop!"

Mister Magister stepped closer, reached out with his hand to touch her shoulder.

"Then it has," he said slowly, softly.

"What?" Stella was not sure what he had said. Could it possibly mean what she thought it might?

"You have done it, young one. It is quite simple, really. By your caring, you have stopped it. Caring is a power far greater than you could know."

"I can't believe it." She fought down a swelling

pressure in her throat, a soaring, bursting feeling in her chest. Stella felt dazed, as though awakening from a bizarre dream. She watched as Magister turned from her and began packing up his rifles, boarding up the back counter of the gallery.

"I will leave you now," he said. "My business here is done."

Things were happening so fast. She could not grasp the reality of the situation. Was this man, or whatever he was, being honest with her? Could she trust him?

"You're *leaving*? You're really leaving, just like that?"

"Yes," he said, making fast the latches on the fold-up countertop. "I have discovered what I came for."

"And what was that?" she asked.

Turning from his work, Magister once again stared at her with his uniquely intense gaze. A cool mantle touched her shoulders as she stood her ground.

"Know this, and never wonder why I came," he said with great solemnity. "I came for *you*."

The words were like ice, and she backed away. "For *me*? You're taking me?"

"No, child, I will not take you anywhere. You —and others like you—are needed right here."

As relief washed over her, Magister finished closing up the gallery. There was a sound in the background, the bristling and snorting of the great black stallion, which had magically appeared in that instant. Before hitching up the horse, the strange man turned to address her one final time.

"Your name," he said. "You are called Stella."

"Yes, that's right. Why?"

"You are well named. It means star."

She looked at him and tried to smile as she accepted the compliment. Magister drew close to her, and with a sweep of his caped arm, gestured upward.

"Look, Stella! Look at the natural beauty and power of the night sky. Look at the stars."

She looked up. They were jewels flung upon black velvet.

"You see the awesome magic of the universe," Magister continued. "We are so overwhelmed by its wonder that we forget a most important thing: If we should take away the stars, there would only be . . . the darkness."

EPILOGUE

Stella continued to look skyward, the memory of Magister's voice lingering in her mind; the pressure of his touch upon her shoulder vanished.

Wheeling about, she saw him hitching up the black horse.

"Where are you going?" she said softly.

He remained silent for a time, then looked back at her. "There are always other places, other times."

"Will you ever come back here?"

"Perhaps," answered Magister. "But not for a long, long time. Long after all that you know has been ground into dust. It never ends, you know."

"But *why*?"

Magister performed an all-too-human shrug. "I do not know. Does it matter?"

Stella tried to smile. "No, I suppose it doesn't . . . not really."

He finished his work, then climbed up to the driver's seat. The droopy brim of his hat tilted back, and his pale face burned in the moonlight.

"The moon is high," he said. "Good for traveling."

Stella followed his gaze, glancing up at the bone-white globe, hanging like a lantern above the meadow.

She heard the chinking sound of the wagon's harness, then silence. The wagon and the stallion, Magister himself—all had vanished like smoke.

The meadow, empty and silent, lay purged by the night winds of autumn. The air grew suddenly cool, but she did not mind the chill; it carried the smells of browning leaves and brittle stalks. She took in a deep breath and rejoiced in her solitude.

It had truly been a time of changes.

But now it was time to go home.